W9-CHP-144

3 1265 00769 7834

The Last Chapter

Leila
Abouzeid

The Last
Chapter

A Novel

Translated by Leila Abouzeid
and John Liechety

With an Afterword
by the author

The American University in Cairo Press
Cairo • New York

English translation copyright © 2000 by
The American University in Cairo Press
113 Sharia Kasr el Aini, Cairo, Egypt
420 Fifth Avenue, New York, NY 10018
www.aucpress.com

First published in Arabic in 2000 as *al-Fasl al-akhir*
Copyright © 2000 by Leila Abouzeid
Protected under the Berne Convention

Dar el Kutub No. 7838/00
ISBN 977 424 588 1

Designed by the AUC Press Design Center
Printed in Egypt

Studying with boys was reckoned to be hard, like running up a desert mountain at noon. We'd had so many warnings about getting pregnant that we half believed we could do so just by talking to them; as if we were studying with ghouls. Yet I learned to prefer interaction with men. Not that I found them intrinsically more intelligent. But they did not pick at our minds, since they assumed we were born without them.

1

This gave me an advantage in class, where the brain I was not supposed to have was generally more than a match for the boys. Outside the classroom it was different. There they were dangerous; there was no choice but to fight. In the struggle we learned to dominate, they merely to provoke with their marketplace banter and their crude and cruel tongues. They were led by an older, vulgar guy who had committed his ignorant flesh to the lurid, muscle-bound photographs in the display windows along Mohammed V Avenue.

That is where partition has brought us; to the point where we are two distinct species. Our science teacher told us about some research project in which an ant was introduced into an established colony, only to be thrown out. This is what they are doing to us women. And yet we derive strength from their actions and they only weakness, like spoiled children who cannot get what they want.

One day the director called us into his office, where we found one of them, a loser from who-knows-where, waiting accusingly.

"What have you been playing at?" the director demanded in his thick provincial accent. He indicated the boy, and waited for our confusion to clear.

"*Rien, Monsieur le proviseur.* Nothing." We squirmed and hoped our 'r's had been adequately French.

The director turned to the boy. "Tell them what you've just told me!"

"This one"—he pointed to me—"insulted me. She told her friend there to look at the *brèche-dent* between my teeth."

Anybody but the director could have seen through this ludicrous allegation. The boy was an inept actor performing a part in a bad play. I wondered why someone so young felt compelled to invent such lies. I must admit that his attempt at sophisticated French, in particular the use of an unfamiliar word to describe a common gap between the teeth, threw me off a second. I guessed its meaning from context, and now the phrase *brèche-dent* is a permanent part of the furniture of my mind, along with images of that incident I would prefer to forget. This is how I understand much language. Even my Arabic vocabulary is taken from usage rather than erudition, which is why I don't have a precise understanding of terms.

What happened next is not important. What is important is what the story about the ants tells us. In those days they rejected us decisively, not as they came to do later, with "an iron hand in a velvet glove." Small wonder then that we were a generation in transition, reaping a botched harvest in its entirety. We were, as the Moroccan saying goes, "the orphans' heads used to train hairdressers."

I am not suggesting that male society is evil and female society good. Hardly! Let's face it, if woman has an enemy it is other women. I learned this the hard way, early on, in that last year of high school.

There were two of us girls in a class of forty-two. (The

3

capacity of the Moroccan classroom is limitless, like that of the Moroccan second-class bus.) Even now I can only refer to her as 'the other one,' even though at first we helped each other stay afloat in that inhospitable sea of boys.

I had not bought the textbook on Islamic thought because 'the other one' had a copy, and we shared everything. Once she had finished using it to prepare for our final exams, I took the book home. I had hardly stepped in the door when the bell rang. Her brother was standing there saying, "My sister wants the book back, now!" I was still holding it, and was stunned, as if by electricity. He snatched it from my hand, and tripped off down the staircase into the street. Still in shock, I listened to his motorbike fart off out of earshot.

The book, *Duha al-Islam* by Ahmad Amin, was a standard reference at the public library, but only instructors could check it out, and since the two days left until the exams were holidays, there was no way I could use it in the library. What could I do? Resign myself to failing in my strongest subject? The thought of repeating that dismal class made me cringe. If I prayed for anything, it was for God to cripple the villain with typhoid fever. Women! What idiot said that they were made of sugar and spice?

I went out in a daze. I was learning to appreciate a saying that experience has made dear to me: "God protect me from my friends, and I'll take care of the enemies!" Friendship is fairytale at best, at worst a bald old lie. The only real friends are children, as long as they remain children.

I found myself, don't ask me how, before the Islamic-thought teacher, and blurted out the whole story. He got me to calm down. Even then I sensed my superiority, that with it I could claim my rights, and crush the enemy.

"We'll go to the library," he said. "I'll sign the book out." That was what I had come for, and I was grateful. I still am, and intend to testify on that instructor's behalf on the Day of Judgment. But I buried trust in women then and there. As I made my way home, I felt as if I were coming from a funeral. Maybe friendship between women is impossible in this country. It was dead for me, at any rate. When the exam results came out, 'the other one' withdrew, defeated and disappointed, as if my success had been her failure.

Why do human beings delight in hurting others? I think of Mademoiselle Doze, a teacher of French I had at the girls' school. She was impregnable as a mountain, yet all of a sudden went to pieces. She started coming to work in a green raincoat, buttoned to the throat, which she never took off.

She was tall and slim with white skin and dark, shining hair tied back in a bun. She rarely raised her voice, a glance alone was sufficient to command an instantaneous stir of activity. Then one day, as if some gate had broken, one girl after another stepped free and started banging desks or dancing about the room in the middle of a lesson. Mademoiselle Doze cowered behind her desk, terrorized and defeated, until the director burst in to restore order.

Mademoiselle Doze was gone, just her body went on showing up for class, wrapped in its raincoat, its lips still painted deep red.

Can you lose your identity the way you lose an identification card? Does some unseen part in the machinery of the self snap, suddenly and irreparably? People said she had been jilted by her fiancé because she had tuberculosis. But how could that have been? She would never have stayed to finish the year if she had had tuberculosis. No one will ever know the truth. I felt sad for Mademoiselle Doze, even if she was French.

As I've said, she rarely raised her voice; only twice to my knowledge. She once surprised a student scratching her scalp intently. Mademoiselle gripped the desk and exploded. "Scratch your filthy head at home!" She was frustrated to be sowing her native tongue on such stony ground, to be sure, but such an outburst confirmed the loathing and innate racism eating at her soul.

On another occasion, a girl came in and sat down with her coat and scarf on. Mademoiselle Doze threw a fit and thoroughly humiliated the girl. Ironic, for someone who would shortly be showing up for work in her raincoat.

Mademoiselle Doze had a soft spot for any student who could fit in to her colonialist notions of civilization. She adored Fatna, a girl who had picked up French as if she had been born in the heart of Paris rather than in one of Rabat's worst shanty towns. How Fatna got to school every day, where she ate lunch, how she maintained her poise, even elegance, these were mysteries to us.

Anyway, the *Duha al-Islam* textbook episode taught me about the trap of friendship, and I have not fallen into it since. Back in the days of Mademoiselle Doze, however, I was still innocent and had made a close friend of a girl named Latifa. She was from Fes, and a descendent of the Prophet, the daughter of a wealthy landowner. That made him a 'feudalist,' and therefore a bad person and enemy of the proletariat, to use some of the popular jargon of the time. Thank God I was young and uninitiated enough to take Latifa for the person she was, rather than through the ludicrous filter of Marxist abstractions.

Latifa's father had come out publicly against corruption, but he was still accused by the socialists of plotting "to swallow every small landowner in the area." What did they expect him to do, sit around like some eccentric or saint doling out his holdings to the poor? And then what? What would adding a square foot of dirt to that multitude of peasant plots have accomplished?

"What's better?" I asked Malika, another friend. "Having a hundred poor devils or a hundred and one? Look what they've done to the Soviet Union!"

"At least there people aren't bitter! Better than nothing!" Malika would spit back through tightened lips. "If everyone's in the same boat, there's nothing to resent, even if it leaks."

I tried to counter her vengeful spirit with the words of

our Prophet: "You cannot have faith until you wish for your brother what you wish for yourself."

"Keep religion out of it!" she hissed.

Why are some hearts closed? What does it mean when even Arabs close their ears to the wisdom of the Prophet's words? Such people deserve to stew in their own bile.

After graduation, I realized I'd got all my vocabulary from the context, so I bought a bunch of dictionaries and set out to teach myself. "Man:" said one, "the summit of the animal kingdom." What more could you ask for? Some years later the gap-toothed guy, who had got a Ph.D. in anthropology, was telling me how humans and animals exhibit the same behavior when they fight. Biologically, they are just the same.

But back to Latifa. Latifa was the product of a pure Fesi family, with all that entails, right down to her fair features and refined tastes. She was not much of a student, but what did that matter when you had money, beauty, and culture? I did not think in those terms at the time. She was simply my friend, whom I accepted without thought. If I look back, however, it is easy to pick out the signs of how it would go wrong. With her gaiety went frivolity, with her elegance moral depravity, with her boldness arrogance.

When Mademoiselle Doze would call the girl sitting next to her to the board, Latifa would steal and eat her snack. She would sit back in her corner, doing whatever she could get away with. At recess she would just laugh in the angry girl's face, a heedless, indifferent laugh that splashed like a waterfall.

Latifa wore her shirts backward, zipper in front, and when anyone mentioned it, she would counter, "Who says it has to be in the back? Is there a law?"

Even worse, she smoked cigarettes, the only one at school who dared. It was no surprise that she dropped out. No one really expected her not to. She did not even get a high-school certificate, the lowest aspiration for a girl of her social standing.

"What's so special about a certificate?" she would ask. "Is it a Mercedes or something? What the hell would I do with it?" She must have gotten her practical sense from her father, who was a well known politician despite being illiterate. She was right. What did she need a diploma for?

I ran into her on several occasions after she quit school. Once she stopped her red convertible and ran across the street to greet me. The magnificent outfit, the same splashing laugh, the joy in her eyes, the poise, the hair, the expensive perfume . . . . She ran back to the car and shot off like an arrow, tires screeching, her arm lifted to me in a wave, her long fair hair to the wind. She ran at life with wide-open arms. Why did God not protect you, Latifa, from red sport cars and all that babbling happiness?

That was the last time I saw her before the scandal. Her father disowned her for marrying a French divorcé with three children. How do you go about declaring that you are no longer the father of your child? You cannot cut that knot with scissors. Latifa's father had her removed from the family records. He used his money and influence to have them rewritten. Then he found a pair of notaries willing to draft a document stating that Latifa was not his blood daughter, that he had got her from an orphanage.

Her mother backed his claim. She was told that if she did not, she would be repudiated as well. To top it all, his parting words to Latifa were, "How in the world did you turn out to be such a slut?"

"I got it from you," Latifa replied, "and one of these days I'll prove it."

Some time later I saw her walking along the street.

"Where're you going in such hurry?" I asked.

"To work! I'm a secretary at the law school!" Latifa? A secretary? She still had all the old radiance and poise, and her French had become impeccable.

They say she lived with the foreigner for a few years. Then poof! He vanished, went back to his wife and children in France. And we Moroccans think foreigners are incapable of such behavior! Apparently she challenged her father and his phony documents in court, and lost. With both parents' testimonies against her, she did not have a case.

Latifa got her revenge, or so they say, by becoming a belly dancer. All Rabat got to admire photos of her fair Fesi flesh in a cabaret window. Then she started dating her father's friends. What a whore! That's what they say. Disgused as a prostitute, she audaciously planted herself along her father's path, and he took the bait. She got into the car, took off her wig and dark glasses, smiled, and said, "Well, now that you know how I got to be such a slut, shouldn't we call your father so he can disinherit you?"

I saw her once or twice more; then she disappeared. The last time was awful. She was wearing dirty beige trousers, a dull braid hung down her back. She had on hiking boots, and shuffled listlessly up the street. Our eyes met. Hers were like dead stars, absent, feeble. They registered without a flicker, without any change. As if she didn't recognize me, as if she had lost all touch with the world around her. She had become dirty, ugly, disgusting. God have mercy! That radiant dignity turned to darkness. God have mercy on her soul. Latifa shuffled out of my life, leaving only her broken image.

What a story! "Were it written with needles on the inner corners of the eye, it would be a lesson for those who would be taught."

I mentioned that the gap-toothed fellow returned from the past. I opened the door and there he was. His face seemed familiar but I could not place it. I tried, but my memory of him had been erased, as in one of Ionesco's plays where a man who has been dead for thousands of years can remember nothing of his former life, save a stone bench somewhere with dead leaves whirling around it.

"You don't know me?" said the face. A dimensionless

11

face, blank as an empty crossword puzzle. "I am al-Raddad! Our senior year!"

"Oh yes, Of course!" I could picture him now, struggling to do justice to his 'r's.

"I'm back from America. I've been feeling the need, it's an obsession really, to look you up. It's strange. I can't explain it."

"A lot of things in life are inexplicable."

"Then you know more or less what I mean?"

"Yes. I think so. Come in! It's happened to me too. A few years back I looked all over Morocco for someone I wanted to find. Come in!"

The image of the old al-Raddad (a skinny body in tired clothes, an unhealthy complexion and crooked nose, scraggy blond beard, the infamous gap-teeth, the vulgarity, arrogance, and insolence) faded. In its place stood a sober, middle-aged man.

He started to take his shoes off. I tried to dissuade him but he insisted, saying, "We're Moroccans. The least we can do is mind our manners." I watched as he placed the shoes neatly by the rug. His shoulders were stooped, his head was bald now, but the fringe of hair remaining at the base was black.

"So you forgot me, did you?"

"Forgetfulness isn't a sin."

"It was for Adam. He lost paradise." He sat on a cushion and smiled at his remark. I smiled too, to be hospitable.

"Do sit over here. It's more comfortable."

"I'm fine where I am," he answered, crossing his legs. I sat on the cushion opposite, while he excused himself in Arabic, using a western expression. "I'm sorry to have come unannounced." I noticed he had had his teeth fixed.

"Not at all. This is Morocco. You are always welcome. Besides, it's not every day the past comes back." I realized my mistake as I spoke. The man in front of me was not from the past. The mark on his forehead attested that he did his prayers regularly. There was a religious humility about him, but his beard was shaved.

"Yes, I've changed," he said reading my thoughts.

"In America?"

"Yes. In America where the dream includes its share of nightmares. I got married, had children, got divorced . . . . I lived in mansions and in slums worse than any of Casablanca. I stayed in luxury hotels, and in shelters for the homeless. I let my children slip away. I lost them." I marveled at these things, as I sensed was appropriate. "I built my castles in the air," he went on. "Anice, my ex-wife, wanted us to get rich quick, and we started speculating in real estate. We'd arrange a loan to buy property, then sell. Before long we had it made. We had our big house and pool."

"I know," I interrupted, "I met an anthropologist who had studied the dreams of Moroccan and American children. Moroccan kids just want to grow up, get married and have a family. American kids want a palace and the pool."

13

"Anice and I turned into American children, but even that wasn't enough. Skin-color got in the way. I couldn't change my features. We never really joined the establishment. We were like people trying to make a hit at a party where everyone knew we hadn't been officially invited."

"And Reagan claimed it was impossible to go to Japan and integrate into the culture, but that anyone could go to the States and become American?"

"It's a myth. Look at the blacks. They've been there five centuries and still don't feel American. I got to know one at the mosque. He would close his eyes and say, 'I want to go home!' I would ask, 'Where's home?' and he would point to the sky. 'Up there! America isn't my homeland, I don't even have a place to call my own here.' Many things became clear to me during my time there, one of which was that we have racism too, but we don't call it that."

"What are you talking about? What do you mean?"

"Yesterday I witnessed a scene on the bus that might have been in America. There was a little black girl, with afro hair and a runny nose. When her mother turned to her and said, 'Get up Gazelle, we're getting off here,' a drunk behind her repeated her name in astonishment, and took the child by the scruff of the neck saying, 'You call her Gazelle? This? How could you so abuse the name? She's not a gazelle, she's a little goat. I'm not going to put her down until you call her Goat.' The woman began to cry. 'I'm warning you,' said the drunk. 'I won't put her down until you say it.' So she said it, the poor woman, through her sobs, and he let the little girl go with the words, 'Get off Gazelle, you little brat, may God curse your parents.' If that scene had happened in the US we'd have called it racism, but because it happened here, we don't give it a name."

"You want to judge us by the words of a drunk?"

"How often do we hear the truth on the lips of a drunk? *In vino veritas*, isn't that what they say?" Al-Raddad's voice had started to tremble.

"I'll make some tea," I said, to distract him.

"With mint? . . . With *sheeba*? You don't happen to have any *sheeba* do you? I haven't had tea with *sheeba* in twenty years." He sighed. "Do you know what I missed the most?" he paused as if he had asked a riddle.

"*Sheeba*?"

"Well, yes. But what else?"

"Homemade bread?" I ventured. He shook his head and waited. Teasingly I said, "*Cardoon*? Everybody misses *cardoon*. They say it exists only in Morocco, like *djellabas*."

He went on shaking his head and smiling.

"I don't know. I give up."

"The sight of old men holding bunches of fresh mint, shuffling down some empty street early in the morning . . . ." He had tears in his eyes now. "Life teases us the way a cat does a mouse before killing it."

"Well, who would've thought that you would emigrate?"

"Who would've thought that any Moroccan would do it?

My father, bless his soul, died in his village without seeing even Casablanca."

"People today don't have much choice."

"I guess not. New York's had its Irish and Italians. Now it's getting Moroccans."

"I had a neighbor once who was ecstatic when his son got a US visa. Better than a Ph.D.! Are you back for good?"

"No! No! Where am I supposed to go?"

"I'm going to make that tea now."

When I came back with the tray he was going on as if he had never stopped.

"And so when the recession hit we couldn't sell the houses and we ended right back where we started."

"Life in America is full of ups and downs."

"We lost everything, our dreams . . . the marriage. My life is a failure."

"Just twenty years of it," I said meaning to cheer him up, but he became even gloomier.

"Failure in a foreign land is a blow you don't get over. I could easily have become one more of their homeless statistics, sleeping in doorways."

I thought of a man from Tangier who had emigrated to the United States in his youth, joined the army, fought in the Korean War, married an American woman, and returned years later, an old lunatic for all his trouble. Naturally I kept that memory to myself and asked al-Raddad, "What took you to the States in the first place?"

"Destiny, I guess. Studies. Didn't I tell you I have a Ph.D. on how similar human beings and animals are in the way that they fight? It's a scientific fact."

"And then you went into business."

"You don't get rich doing post-graduate work. Not even in America."

"I guess Anice wouldn't have wanted you to be an academic."

"And don't forget how competitive it is, and my being a foreigner."

"But there are Arab professors with good university jobs."

"I knew this Palestinian at my university. He stayed in school twenty years. He couldn't get a real job, and he couldn't stay on unless he was a student. He survived by mowing lawns, painting houses. When the visa was ready to expire he'd just register for more coursework."

"Brave new world of the Arab Muslim!"

"He wasn't even Muslim, he was Christian. And that's not the end of the story. When the peace negotiations started, he went home to visit his mother for the first time, and died a few days later in his sleep. I read about it in a department newsletter. They called him an expert on Palestinian affairs in spite of his twenty years in exile. They said he was a 'modest and pragmatic' man, his reward, I guess, for twenty years of post-graduate study. And what do you suggest I do with my Ph.D. on the animal aggression of man?"

"If you had stayed here, you'd be a dean by now or . . ."

"A minister." He interrupted. "Well, we don't decide our

fate. What's done is done." He gestured to emphasize his words. "We can't go back and fix our mistakes. If I had known then what I know now, I'd never have left my country."

"No matter what?"

"What's the point of contributing to a 'progress' in the name of others? You might as well stay home and achieve nothing, at least it's your own nothing. One hand can't . . . ? How does the saying go?"

"What's the sound of one hand clapping?" I suggested.

He nodded.

"But you can make plenty of noise with a slap. And we're good at that," I said.

He laughed.

"You've still got the creative touch." He said "That's what people envied in you."

I thought of him back in the director's office, that scrawny, screwed-up little boy pointing his accusing finger at me. I sensed that the new al-Raddad was thinking of it too. He responded with warmth, as if to draw my mind off the topic.

"People used to say how in sixth grade you would write 'A' papers for the tenth graders. They used to say that your teacher would lock his room when he graded your papers, because he didn't want anyone catching him using a dictionary."

I smiled to be reminded of those stories.

"Each one of us has natural gifts. Unfortunately, we destroy them in each other."

"With slaps?"

"Among other things. Did you know that Egyptian film stars come to Morocco to consult our scholarly expertise?"

"In Islam?"

I snorted. "In spells and magic! But let's not get into that now. I wouldn't want to spoil your visit. We're Muslims by birth, nothing more, as someone said. I'll tell you a joke but you mustn't repeat it." He was listening intently now. "When Musa ibn Nussair conquered Morocco and presented Islam to the people, they said, 'We'll think about it.'"

"Well?"

"Thirteen hundred years later they're still thinking."

"My mother used to say, 'Corruption and adultery aside, Moroccans are highly virtuous.' Meaning of course that we're nothing of the sort." His mother could hardly have said this in the refined Arabic her son was using. I would have preferred the bawdier version. "Is that what you're talking about?"

"That, and bribery and . . . a host of other calamities here in your idyllic Morocco," I answered.

"Our Morocco," he retorted.

"*Their* Morocco, actually. Their Morocco is crawling with fortune-tellers and sorcerers. It's worse than *The Arabian Nights*. The only power women have is through witchcraft. It is their only trump card."

"Is it just women?"

"Men too."

"And where does Islam fit in? God have mercy!" His intensity startled me. And he repeated himself over and over again, until I wished he would let up. Then he intoned a prayer, powerful and sad, that moved us both to tears.

Where had he learned to pray like that? In America? What a transformation! Could this really be the same sallow wretch who had once planted lies against me? And why was he watching me now?

"You still have your Arabic," I said. In truth, although the prayer had been lovely, he spoke Arabic with a slight foreign accent, often searching for the right word, and resorted to English whenever he felt unsure of how to express himself. My compliment pleased him. He returned a grateful, if somewhat incredulous smile.

"Language is a skill. You use it or lose it, but it's coming back since I've been going to the mosque. Do you ever hear from your classmate? What was her name again?"

"She's still alive," I answered. "She lives here in Rabat but I don't see her. Has half a dozen kids. I guess I did see her once. She looked like someone coming up from underground, completely out of touch, buried in marriage."

"Do you know that story about the peasant who came down from some remote village in the mountains to find Marrakech buzzing with news of the sultan's return from exile?"

"No. What happened?"

"Well, naturally he asked, 'What's all the excitement?'

and they told him, 'The sultan is back!' 'Good lord!' said the peasant. 'I didn't even know he'd left.'"

I laughed, and recounted how 'the other one' had dropped by unexpectedly, just as al-Raddad had done. She'd come to see where I had gotten in life. She admitted as much. "You read, you travel, you're growing. I do nothing. I've got nothing to offer."

"I'm the one who's supposed to be envying you," I said.

"For what?"

"Six children. God alone knows what any of them might accomplish some day." She was not convinced. When it was time to go, she got up on child-thickened legs, and tottered heavily away.

"Women nowadays want to have children and careers, to have their cake and eat it too," observed al-Raddad.

"It can't be done here," I said.

"Or any place else. What about you? Do you have children?" Ah. There it was at last! Do I have children? What he meant was, "Are you married?"

"No." I said. "I am not married." He sat there waiting for more. Twenty years in the States hadn't smoothed off the rough edges completely. "No, I'm not married. That's what you meant, isn't it? Like asking a writer who her favorite author is when what you really want to know is who shaped her style?" I was trying to divert him, but he dived back in.

"Why not? You have had many admirers, myself included."

Make yourself right at home, I thought. Take your shoes

off, al-Raddad. So I now have the privilege of counting you among my male 'admirers'? Is that why you had me called in to face the director? What had looked to me like jealous spite appeared now to have been merely 'admiration' on his part. This is how Moroccan men relate to Moroccan women. Love is war. Marriage is war.

"It's true. I was desperately in love with you." Easy to say, now that it belongs to the past. "I really can't believe you're still single." Damn marriage anyway! What had he got out of it? How could he still extol the virtues of a thing at which he'd so thoroughly failed?

"I did try," I said. "As a Muslim I believe that we're here as God's representatives on earth, and that having children is a part of that duty. It hasn't worked out. Whenever I've got close, the whole thing has fallen apart."

"But why?"

I was growing weary of this conversation.

"God knows."

"It's odd! Perhaps it was written or perhaps you were under some sort of spell."

The Ph.D. and swimming pool evidently hadn't delivered him from his capacity for such analyses.

"You sound like a real Moroccan."

"I suppose I do. Listen to this. The same year I married Anice, this girl from Fes married an American. I couldn't figure out what an American man could possibly see in a Moroccan woman, and I told him as much. 'How could you give up an American girl for a Moroccan? You're out of your mind!' Those were my words."

"No prophet is honored in her own house," I said.

"This feels like a therapy session or something. I have never told these things to any one before."

"Well, it's a good thing you're in Morocco then, isn't it?"

"Incidentally, that girl from Fes has forgotten Arabic entirely. She can't even interpret for visitors who don't speak English. And when I told her how I missed Morocco, about the old men holding their bunches of mint, she accused me of clinging to the past. 'Everyone misses their country.' I told her. 'You must too.' 'I miss nothing about Morocco. Absolutely nothing. This is my country now.'"

"I suppose she has her reasons." I said.

"Her father."

"He was hard on her?"

"And how. He'd come home and beat on the door like a madman, until she came terrified to ask who it was. 'It's me,' He'd scream. 'You open this door or I'll open your head, by God!' She cried as she told the story, twenty years later."

"Too bad her father isn't over there. She could sue him for child abuse. What a story! Were it written with needles on the inner corners of the eye, it would be a lesson for those who would be taught."

"What's that?" He looked bewildered.

"An old way of speaking. It's from *The Arabian Nights*."

"It's surrealism. Have the Arabs been surrealists for so long, then?"

"That's why no one takes them seriously."

"Arab politicians, you mean?"

"I mean Arabs. Take a typical mother talking to her kids: 'If you don't shut up, I'll kill you, I swear I will in God's name!'"

"How did we get on to this topic?"

"You were telling me about your Fesi friend, and I thought of *The Arabian Nights*."

"Oh, right!"

"I know why you didn't fit in America, because you didn't despise your life in Morocco enough." Then I remembered what he had said about losing his children. It is always the children who pay. I remembered a Lebanese friend from my student days in the States, a fundamentalist, no less, who announced one day, "I'm marrying an American girl. I'd like you to meet her."

I was stunned. I had not dreamed such a thing was conceivable for someone professing his brand of religion. "Well, what do you think?"

"I thought you said your mother was finding a bride for you in Beirut. If you really want my opinion, let her do it, a Muslim girl would be better for you."

"Why better?" he shot back defensively. How was I supposed to tell a fundamentalist why a Muslim wife made sense? An American girl had been sufficient to shake his presumably unshakable faith. Why was he asking me, a Muslim woman, for advice if he could not concede even that I had the virtue of being marryable. I stated the obvious.

"A Muslim wife would be better for you," I said, "because of your religion." He probably did not even know if his bride-elect was a Christian or a Jew. He stared at the ground as he ususally did in my female presence.

"I'll make her a Muslim." I wanted to laugh in his face, but he was still looking down.

"Why should she give up her religion for you? Would you give up yours for her?"

"Don't be ridiculous."

"Then why take it for granted that she would?"

"My religion is better than hers."

"Maybe she says the same thing."

"Are you telling me not to marry her?"

"I'm not telling you anything. I'm saying what I think."

"Don't worry. I know what I'm doing."

"I worry about your children not you."

That seemed to deflate him, and he came up with a story that supported my argument, about a fundamentalist friend of his who'd been married to an American for a long time. "They celebrate Halloween," he concluded, as if he had just pulled the pin on a grenade and thrown it.

"Oh my!" I said.

"They say it's just another holiday. It's devil worship if you ask me! Just like rock music with its blasphemous beat and lyrics and performers. It's satanic, but no one seems to be aware of it. Anyway, my friend is the only one who fasts during Ramadan. The rest of the family lie around eating pork and drinking beer. I recently attended a birthday party there. The youngest daughter was kissing her boyfriend right in front of her father!"

"No doubt your friend intended to turn his wife into a good Muslim once." I remarked, knowing full well that it little mattered what I said. Had I known al-Raddad's story then, I'd have thrown it in for good measure. I turned back to my guest abruptly. He too had been absorbed in his own thoughts.

Before long, he was on his feet slipping into his shoes. He said goodbye somewhat perfunctorily, and made his way down the staircase. I locked the door, and he returned to the past.

2

The relationship with Salim had never been publicly declared, but people knew about it. I am thankful God does not always grant our wishes in these cases. Had it ended in marriage, Salim would have planted his quota of children and run out on me. I soon grew disillusioned with him. It was like learning that what you thought to be a precious stone was cheap glass after all. Now my youth is gone, and I still haven't found a diamond.

Husbands in our country are born with an instinct for betrayal. Betraying a mate is as bad as high treason in my opinion. Yet look how we condemn a traitor to the nation while a man who betrays his wife and family is absolved. "It's his nature," we shrug. Meanwhile, we jump to ostracize a woman guilty of the slightest transgression.

I recall a time when I was going abroad. An older woman sat next to me in the airport. She was tall and slim, with a clear complexion and a tattoo down her chin. She bore the traces of Bedouin beauty you only encounter in the Moroccan countryside. She asked if I would help her find her gate, then started to talk. Our women are so burdened with grief they will seize any moment to lighten the load.

She was observing an old couple. The man was holding his wife's arm and carrying her coat. They were foreigners, most likely Europeans. "Look at that," sighed my companion. "They could be friends. They could be brother and sister. Have you ever seen a Moroccan couple their age looking like that?"

"Are you kidding? I've seen them at each other's throats, though."

"A wife starts looking tired, and that's the signal for her husband to marry a newer model, and start in on some more children."

"Foreigners take an oath when they marry, you know. They promise to be true 'for better or for worse, in sickness and in health, till death us do part,' or something like that."

Again she sighed. "Mine left me with seven children before he took another wife." Why would it take seven children to figure out your wife was inadequate? "He married a girl young enough to be his daughter. He admitted she only married him for his money. He was proud of it."

"You say she was young. She must have been shrewd too."

"Oh, yes! My children were pushed aside without a penny. Not one of them has so much as finished school."

"And that doesn't bother their father?"

"She destroyed his sense of judgment."

"How so?"

"She bewitched him," the woman replied, as if to say 'what else?' "She put a spell on him, my dear. She's an expert. The devil himself isn't much better. May God do his worst with her!"

"Well what about you? Can't you protect yoursef with spells of your own?"

"I try. Hers are stronger."

If you both keep this up, I thought, you'll drive the old bastard insane. "Well," I said, "a woman can make a man lose his grip on reality, I guess. It's happened before."

"She's young and pretty, he's bent in half like a hunchback."

"What a travesty! It's worse than that. It's legalized adultery. He ought to be in jail," I put in.

"He's getting 'younger.' He's dying his hair and getting massaged twice a week. My boys told him he ought to be ashamed of himself and he said, 'What for? Don't I have the right to enjoy my life?' Then he started hacking his lungs out. 'It was written as my destiny the day I was born. Why should we meddle with what God ordains?'"

I told the story to Salim. "The old buzzard did what he did and called it fate," I said. "Another man who thinks with his testicles, and blames it on his religion." I felt like adding that it had always been like this, all through Arab history, but I remembered the day I had given to Salim a collection of al-Mutanabbi's poems, and I cut myself short. "Put it by your bed," I had suggested, handing him the work. "It'll help you remember your native tongue. Even Christians in the Middle East know Arabic better than we do, and they were colonized by the French too." I was referring to the letters he'd been writing me in French. "We're rootless," I went on. "The weakest current carries us away. How could just forty years of the French have done so much harm? What if they'd been in Morocco as long as they were in Algeria? They weren't even interested in teaching us. Good grief! If a Moroccan spends a night in Cairo, he wakes up speaking fluent Egyptian."

Salim was leafing through the book. "I'm not sure I can handle al-Mutanabbi all in one go," he said. "He's out of my league."

"Just put it on your bedstand to remind you that there are other languages besides French. French is a foreign language, remember."

"So is Arabic for me," he said with the trace of a smile.

The truth of his words hit home, and I acknowledged it immediately. "Arabic is not the language of the Berbers," he repeated.

"But it's still the language of their religion. And you've seen how men behave! They've been like this throughout Islamic history." I used the word 'Islamic' to include him.

Salim laughed, and said, "It's reactionism!"

So now he was getting into politics was he? He never missed that opportunity. Then he added, solemnly, almost ceremoniously, "Education is the answer. With education we'll turn ignorance into knowledge, superstition into faith."

What is this faith they talk about, anyway? Isn't it just another of the words they use to bribe the masses? It did not really matter what I said to Salim. If I mentioned al-Raddad's lies or the perfidious behavior of 'the other one,' he would pronounce his mantra: "It's reactionism! Progress will turn hatred into love, and transform this society." And then of course: "Education is the key."

Salim made a fair copy of his leader. He had the same tone, gestures, frown. He used the same stock phrases, but a copy he remained, nonetheless, lacking the authenticity and the value of the original.

I had seen the leader in person once. Salim had taken me to one of his lectures. He was short and conservatively dressed, with thick eyebrows that met in the middle. He had lost some hair which added to his air of intelligence. His face projected the strength of his convictions, the depth of his energy, the pragmatic clarity of his mind.

Although the leader had had a French education, he spoke in Arabic. Much of what he said came out like translations of French expressions. I felt that I was missing the point he was making, and decided to take notes. When I went back to them later, I realized that the speech had been fascinating in spite of the poor Arabic in which it was delivered, and that the leader was, in his way, exceptionally devoted to his country. Here is the speech, as far as I can reconstruct it:

Our self-contempt is a by-product of culture shock. In times past we belittled the West, and isolated ourselves behind thick walls. Prior to colonization, these fortresses of ours turned back not only invaders, but progressive ideas as well. It was not until the beginning of this century that the colonizers managed to penetrate those walls.

They found craftsmen and peasants working long hours, using antiquated methods. These workers tended to be narrow-minded, neglecting their children's health and education in the pursuit of their daily bread. In short they found a society that was, in the idiom of political scientists, 'underdeveloped,' a situation the colonizer did nothing to change.

Moroccan society had become stagnant. The traditional disciplines had deteriorated to the point where their socalled masters were mere parrots of informtion. Mathematics sacrificed logic and reason for a silly set of hollow incantations used for calculating prayer times. Science was monopolized by a narrow elite, who withheld their knowledge, thereby extinguishing it.

Another sign of Morocco's underdevelopment can be seen in the proliferation of shrines and sects. Annual festivals sprang up around the tombs of patriots and saints. With them came a wave of religious charlatans, spurious brotherhoods, and superstitious awe.

The colonizer perpetuated these diseases and archaisms, turning our country into a museum. This tendency is exemplified by Boniface [a French ruler of Morocco during the protectorate] and his circle's opposition to our plans to modernize the Qarawiyin University in Fes. They claimed that such modernization was not in keeping with Islam, as if they had any authority in such matters.

While the colonizers had no interest in awakening the political awareness of the Moroccan people, it was growing stronger nonetheless. Foreign journalists were often surprised to find a radio set in a shack that was lucky if it held a bed. Ironically, by his very intention to stifle it, the colonizer played a key role in developing our political awareness.

The conservative religious movement reacted by showing flexibility vis à vis modernism. We began to remove the layers of superstition caked upon our Islamic heritage. If not for such a movement, our young people studying overseas would surely have abandoned their religion.

Finally, Moroccans working in the colonizer's factories were becoming conscious of their rights. There was a growing socio-political awareness; nevertheless, our society was in bad shape before and during colonization.

Since independence, our mission has been to build a new society. We must consider first the welfare of our citizens. And we must reclaim for our nation a vibrant international role and a chance to contribute to intellectual and scientific progress.

The raw materials for change are already with us, (demographic power, political awareness, laborers to do the job); all that remains is to plot the best course. We must not content ourselves with the superficial fruits of change. Trading a *fes* for a topee, trading Arabic for French; this is not what we mean by 'change.' Have we fought for independence, have we come so far, merely to be content with trinkets? Certainly not! We have fought so that our citizens may reap the true fruit of independence, namely: well-being, justice and knowledge for all, and economic, intellectual and social progress for the entire country.

We cannot escape the fact of poverty. The standard of living is low, fair wages are practically nonexistent, especially in rural areas. A key reason for this is our dependence on agriculture, which provides a quarter of the national income, and is the only means of survival for three-quarters of the population.

How can we put an end to poverty? By developing agriculture out of its current primitive state, by developing industry and distributing the resultant wealth evenly among the population. "If there is food better feed all," says a Chinese proverb. Our government would do well to take note, and build a more just system of taxation.

The government can encourage agricultural cooperatives, and supply them with financial and technical assistance. Peasants must learn cooperation, not competition. Old boundaries will be changed to allow modern equipment access to the fields. How can we expect to be productive, when each peasant must hack at a piece of dirt with inadequate tools, hoping against hope for rain?

And of course, our country is underdeveloped because of the neglect to education. The training of teachers and technicians is not enough. We must reform and revitalize the system from the inside. A real country is not built on externals, on fireworks and military parades, rather on the work of its scholars, engineers, and researchers. These are the people whose quiet strength makes it possible to turn the corner from servitude to liberation.

Out of some two thousand engineers in this country, only two hundred are Moroccan. If we look at nations in a similar plight, we will see three conditions that have to be met if we are to find a way out:

1. Political leadership must earn the people's respect through integrity and competence.

2. Economic, social, and political strategies must be clearly drawn and carried out.

3. The people must play a part in developing these strategies, through democratically elected institutions at every level.

If one of these conditions is not met, all must fail. And we know they are not being met. Nothing short of a revolution will make them meet! A coup is necessary, a coup to cleanse our own political system. We must act with the same revolutionary spirit that stirred our people in the struggle against colonialism!

The motley audience poured into the streets. A witches' brew of political buzzwords filled the air, 'exploitation,' 'liberty,' 'change,' 'combat,' . . .

"Well," said Salim "What did you think?"

"I think they've caught some sort of political virus."

"I mean about the speech?"

"Oh, that. I need to read over my notes. But I must say, that man's a born leader. He looked like a Russian to me. There aren't many like that in the Third World. He's really something!" I got home with a head full of swirling terminology and images of the leader.

"He's got something special. It's in every gesture he makes," I told Salim a bit later.

"He only sleeps two hours a night."

"Like Napoleon, huh? No time to waste. Our leaders have to act while they can, since they are usually executed before they get anywhere near old age."

Salim was holding a book out for me to look at. It was Baudelaire's *Les fleurs du mal*. This for al-Mutanabbi? Was Salim a pervert as well as a revolutionary? Now he began to speak, as he had on other occasions, about a student in his boarding school who spent his weekends with some old French woman.

"What a man!' I said sarcastically. "Where did he find her?"

"Some tavern or club. Casablanca has everything."

"Poor Casablanca!" I said. "Once the center of the Resistance, now the center of vice."

He laughed, raised a clenched fist, and cried, "First independence, then freedom!" His evident pleasure in that development annoyed me. It was as if a mask had fallen and I was seeing him for the first time. Tall and slim with his pointed chin, his hair and skin a deep brown. His clothes were autumnal in their varying hues of brown. He was lying on one side chewing the end of a grass stem, his dark eyes flashing provocative signals whenever my gaze met his.

Arabs are supposed to find that lazy, lounging posture irresistible, but Salim was no Arab. I didn't even know his origins for sure. I examined him closely. His sharp, triangular face looked like a viper's. Everything about him was dark and enigmatic. Where did he get his subtle command of Moroccan Arabic? What did his father do for a living? Why was Salim still in school? He was old enough to be raising a family.

Salim was still smiling, gnawing the stem of grass, thinking, I could tell, of his latest letter, one of those he had sent over the holidays. He wrote well in French, and as if liberated from the constraints of speech. He wrote honestly and straightforwardly, as if talking to himself. Yet whenever I read the letters, I found myself translating back into Arabic. Language is the most insidious wedge the colonialists have driven into our society.

The letter had begun with the standard "Dear Aisha," and went on to say:

It is nice being home but I miss Rabat. I want to be in both places. This thorny scrub out here turns to paradise every spring, my version of paradise, anyhow. I wish you could see the fields where I sit to write. The hillsides are covered with yellow and orange daisies, set off against the green grass. The fields are spattered with red poppies. It's like an impressionist painting. It makes me go warm and nostalgic. The air is sweet, and breathing it makes me feel young. The French were right to describe Morocco as "planes of color and light." I wonder why it has yet to produce a great poet.

This Morocco is lovely in the spring, the one sure advantage of being in the countryside. I doubt that you would understand, your Morocco being the capital. But anyway, I wouldn't trade our friendship for all this beauty, I wouldn't trade it for the National Bank. Am I waxing poetic? Don't worry, I wouldn't dare attempt it in what you call "the language of the colonialist."

I can see you there, smiling your little obscure smile, half-mocking, half-dubious. There should be no doubt between us. Why have I been seeing you every week for these last two years? Do you ever ask yourself?

My sister was so excited when she saw your picture. What if she'd seen the real thing? I told her about your hair and your mannerisms and all the other things the picture cannot do justice to. My school friends tell me I'm lucky. Don't I know it! "God protect you two from the evil eye," my sister says. But I am not worried. I trust myself, I trust you, I trust life.

Oh, my love . . . .

Well, now, there is a word for you! It took him four paragraphs to get there, but he did, and as far as I was concerned he was asking for trouble. He must have come unhinged sitting amongst the flowers. As for me, back in "my Morocco," my feet at least were firmly on the ground. "Don't trust yourself, don't trust me, and don't trust life!" I wanted to shout it in his ear. As for the declaration that he wouldn't sell my friendship for all the money in the Bank of Morocco, I considered myself fortunate that I knew more clearly perhaps than most people the absolute worthlessness of words.

In four paragraphs he had gone from "my dear" to "my love." At that rate I would end up being "my lover." I decided to nip the thing in the bud. Where had he got this stuff? Was he reading the French tabloids along with Baudelaire? Was he really in love or was he just a country bumpkin showing off his French?

I got a sheet of paper, and whipped off a curt note in French: "What are you talking about when you say, 'My love'? Don't use that word again, or any of the other absurdities you get watching foreign films. Aisha, Rabat. 15 August 1965."

And now he had the audacity to start in on his gigolo friend and the French woman. The mask had decidedly fallen, his intentions were out in the open. What had I seen in this cad? Why hadn't I caught on sooner? What was I doing there?

In a way it appalled me that I was not convinced by him, and never could be. But then, why would anyone take a student seriously in the first place? Love is one thing, conviction another. I desperately needed to get out.

His mask had fallen after two years. Thank God it had not waited till we were married! Marriage has its own kind of truth. They offer you the moon dipped in honey, knowing full well the bitter herbs to follow. Then all that's left for you is patience, which is why they make so much of patience and call it beauty.

I came back to reality. He was still there, leaning on his elbow and chewing his stem. He was just another face now, the splendor, the kindness, the good looks were gone. They had left him the way a soul leaves a corpse.

"Why're you looking at me like that?" He was angry. At least he had a little backbone left. "If you've something to say, say it!" so I said it.

"I heard you danced with the English teacher at the school party." His English teacher was French. My accusation burst out in a torrent. "They say you made an ass of yourself."

He turned pale and stiff, his lip trembled.

"Shit! I know who told you. It was your loyal classmate. Wasn't it? I confess. I danced. So what? We all did."

Everybody? The others at that party had been young enough to be his kids. What was he doing dancing like a European? Where had he learned how? In his village? Was this what he meant by progress? All we seem to learn from the 'developed' world are its trivialities.

"And why should I be the only one forbidden to dance?" he continued. "I don't get it."

"Because we thought you were above it!" I snapped back, in silence. I didn't feel like explaining. It wasn't the dancing, of course, so much as the partner. Dancing today and tomorrow . . . . I knew those French women. They had not come just to give English lessons. I knew the one he had danced with, and she confirmed all my misgivings.

"Doubt has no place between us," to quote Salim. Right! In any case, I knew two people who would be delighted by what had happened, that French dancer for one, but even more so 'the other one.' The news 'the other one' had brought me had lived up to her highest expectations. My relationship with Salim died on the spot. We are a dangerous kind of people. We love and hate and destroy each other in silence.

Salim slithered off along the walls of the city. He could have his illusions if he wanted them, trusting himself, me, life. Presently he dropped out of school and disappeared. I saw him several years later in Casablanca, walking slowly beside an elderly French woman, who supported herself on his arm.

In the sixties I graduated from high school and went on to university. All together there were about ten of us in my department. The year Morocco became independent, 1956, there were reputed to be just six female high school graduates in the whole country, a direct consequence of forty-four years of French rule. The exact number is not important, what is important is that the French so obviously interfered with our education. The modern university able to start only after independence. All we had got from the colonialists in terms of education was a second-rate knowledge of their language.

My years at university were flavorless, colorless and odorless. We girls had a few male colleagues we considered friends. They were for the most part well-behaved, and treated us more or less naturally.

Those nondescript years went, and others came in their place. At work I did my best, as I had at school. I held to the popular saying "Marriage and death are two afflictions one cannot escape." In America, I am told, they say it is death and taxes. One thing is sure, had it not been for my education, I would have been busy producing my half dozen offspring like the average woman of the day. Some had a dozen, not counting the still-births. Small wonder it was marriage that our version of the saying paired with death.

I was twelve when the first suitor turned up. Father sent him packing, believing him insane, or perhaps believing his daughters could stay beyond the reach of the intrusions of men. Father did not use any of the usual excuses, "she's too young," "she needs to finish school," etc. He simply screamed till he turned red and his eyeballs were ready to pop out, then he stalked from the room. Marriage at twelve?

The second suitor came the following year. He was a military man. "I'd like to ask for the hand of your youngest," he said to Father. He meant the oldest. "The one who just opened the door for me," he added, helpfully. The time it had taken him to cross the room had been enough for him to make his decision. He may as well have been shopping for shirts. They will abandon you just as casually, of course. I would like to get inside their minds to see how they work. Whether it is getting married or overthrowing a regime, they act on the same arbitrary impulse. My second suitor eventually died in prison, where he landed after a failed coup.

How strange life is! When I think how but for God's grace and education I could have ended up a teenage widow with a litter of children to bring up! Fortunately, it was the wrong man and the wrong time. But the truth is that it is always the wrong man and the wrong time. Show me a perfect union. Show me one couple who have shaped their reality and not merely surrendered to it. Everyone surrenders, and decides to go on, or not to go on, and in either case they sing the same old tune, "It was written as my destiny"; "We have to hang on for the sake of the children"; "Happiness is in the next world."

These days educated women are not obliged to marry for economic reasons or to satisfy social expectations. Things have changed. Women can choose. Many marry foreigners whom they have met at school or at work, or they miss the boat.

The third suitor turned up at work. This one had a good position and showed glimmers of personality. He was something of an intellectual. At least he was not an out-and-out loser like the others.

He had been born and raised in the mountains near Azrou. Circumstances had made him more at ease with French than with either Arabic or Islam. He was a product of the Azrou School, where they did their best to turn Berber children into French speakers. He certainly came out with a French shell, but his spirit lay hidden like a pearl underneath.

It was always that way. I once met a Moroccan woman who had been raised by nuns at the Agdal Cathedral in Rabat. Although she spoke Arabic, her attitudes and behavior where distinctly un-Moroccan. She told how her husband had left her with a baby. He had accused her of being more Christian than the nuns. "And why shouldn't I be?" she argued to me. "The sisters gave me love and stability. They gave me the freedom to marry a Muslim. He gave me nothing but accusations and the week-old child he walked out on."

A curse on colonialism! Phosphates and tangerines weren't enough. It needed our souls as well. I could see that woman's Christian spirit staring at me from the other side of her eyes. I will never forget it. It sent shivers up my spine. I can see her coming towards me, pushing a pram around a square. She carried herself like a foreigner, but called my name, and started talking in Arabic about how we used to ride the same bus.

"You don't remember me, do you? There was a bunch of us who used to sit at the back. There was that Fesi girl who lived in the policemen's apartment buildings."

I remembered the Fesi but not her. She seemed put out. I tried harder but failed.

"I'm sorry. It has been so long and I have a very poor memory. I often can't even remember what I've just had for lunch."

"I can see that bus as if it were yesterday. All of us girls crammed together in the back . . ."

"I'm sorry."

"You have worn yourself out with your studies," she declared. It was my turn to be put out, but I tried not to show it. She wanted to talk. I let her. I stayed there till dusk blurred the square, till the street lamps and headlights sputtered in the damp Rabat air. I pulled my jacket closer around me, and still she talked, oblivious to night falling, forgetting her quiet child in the carriage.

Back to the third suitor. All he had really gotten from France was the gibberish he spoke, all he had gotten from Islam was his name. When I started working for the ministry he had already been there for quite a while. We spent a year waiting for the other one to say what was on their mind. We would sit together at break, expectantly sipping coffee. He would call me on the phone from his office to wish me good morning. He sent me a post card once.

Dear Aisha,

I am in Seville. From the narrow window in my room I can see the city's whitewashed roofs, the laundry stretched out to dry.

For a minute I thought I was in Fes. The walls and gates make you think you are in Rabat. The tilework is pure Moroccan. If you were here, you would cry to see the lovely world your ancestors had to leave behind.

The Holy Week festivals are all dust and sweat and rank smells, dung and old pork. Donkeys, mules, pictures of witches, the bodyless head you see sometimes in circus sideshows . . . . The Spaniards are still in the middle ages. No wonder they were less arrogant than the French when they were colonizing the northern part of our country. They were just as poor and underdeveloped as we were. I hope you do not consider my remarks xenophobic.

Mohammed

Seville, 26 September 1996.

I had to look up *xénophobie* in a French dictionary. "Xenophobia: hatred of foreigners."

Meanwhile, society produced its usual mutterings: "Twenty-five and still single! When I was twenty-five I had a ten-year-old daughter already."; "Isn't it time to think about having children?"; "Don't wait too long. There may not be anyone left by the time you hit thirty."; "You're not interested in marriage? Then stay single, for all I care!" This last was half-warning, half-condemnation. In spite of the muttering, I refused to settle for anything less than the right man. Say what they would, I had my job. They could not buy my acquiescence.

It was around that time that an American woman called Susan came to Rabat to do research on Moroccan marriages and chose to interview me, among others—Americans will turn anything into a dissertation. I had been telling my story a while, when she asked, "What do you mean by the 'right' man?"

"Someone worth loving." The spontaneity of my reply surprised me. She noticed.

"You seem surprised. Why?"

"The words came out easily in the foreign language." It had not occurred to me before that a foreign language could be liberating.

"Where did your idea of love come from?"

I wanted to sound scientific and matter of fact. The best I could answer was, "From Egyptian movies . . . . From Umm Kulthum's songs. From pre-Islamic poetry. Arabs you know are authorities on love. They aren't so good at saying, 'I love you,' but they're still authorities."

"Tell me about your courtship. Who was the first to say something?" Susan was asking about the man at work.

"Neither one of us, really. It was just that a fourth suitor and his family had showed up to ask my hand by then. At least this formal solicitation forced me to approach my colleague at work and ask him to clarify his intentions. I had to know what he was thinking.

"'I'm glad you've asked,' he said, speaking very deliberately. 'Thank you for raising the subject. The question is highly appropriate at this time . . . .'

"I told him just to get to the point. I wished he could be himself for once, and have his say, even if he had to do it in Berber.

"'As I am an existentialist, marriage, I'm afraid, is not compatible with my philosophy.' I had always considered such 'philosophy' a lot of amoral, nihilistic claptrap. 'I wanted to tell you many times. I was afraid I would lose you. It was my misfortune to be attracted to such a religious person.' Now my faith was being considered a defect.

"'Well, What do you want from me?' I said. I was fuming.

"'I want a free relationship, like the rest of the world.'

"At last it was out. He wanted to live like a moral outcast and call it freedom."

"But hadn't you suspected all of this before?" Susan put in.

"Yes. I suppose so. But I didn't want to admit it. I preferred to go on hoping. I guess I avoided looking at the evidence too closely."

"What did you tell him then?"

"I turned my back on him and walked away. Occasionally we'd pass each other at work. He'd give me a *'Bonjour'* and keep moving. Whatever feeling I had for him had died on the spot."

"Was it the same for him?"

"No. He approached me four years later. He'd been waiting in the corridor. He caught up with me, and burst out that he couldn't forget me and that he'd decided in favor of marriage after all. 'I want . . .' he began and I tossed his French back in his face: 'Perhaps you do but I don't.' He was four years too late. What a life!"

"Well, what about the other one, the guy who'd come with his family to make a formal proposal? You said he was serious about marriage. What happened with him?"

"He was a civil servant, reasonably well educated, and religious. If he had worked out, I would be an official wife at this very moment, shuttling between work and the house, cooking, yelling at children, cleaning, doing laundry and all the rest of it."

"I take it he didn't work out."

"My father used his power of veto. He said he had a better match in mind. There was no discussion."

"Why not? You had a university degree, you had a good job. I would think the decision was at least half yours to make."

"Think again. The worst of it was that my father rated as an 'intellectual.' But believe me, while our male intellectuals love to expound their liberated views in panel discussions or newspaper editorials, in private they're no better than petty dictators. My father's word was as arbitrary as it was final."

"How did it make you feel?"

"Helpless as a slave. My supposed freedom from illiteracy, unemployment, the veil, were a joke, an illusion. I still had a chain around my neck."

"Where was your mother through all of this?"

"I could talk to her. She was sympathetic, but that didn't make her any less of a slave than I was. After the suitor and his family came, my mother sat around in a cold sweat rehearsing what she'd say to my father when he called."

"Your father wasn't in Rabat?"

"No. He lived in Marrakech, where he had a second wife. My mother sat waiting for his call as if it was going to be a police interrogation. All her arguments, all her persuasions, all that rehearsing . . . . When the phone call finally came, and she told him what had happened, all you could hear was my father screaming. She was petrified, as if he might jump out of the receiver. She couldn't stand up to him. He did what he liked.

"Mother came into the living room looking pale and faint. I ran out for some water. The best I could do, for all my degrees and my good position in the ministry, was to sprinkle water on my mother's face. We were in exactly the same boat. When she came back to herself, she just repeated dully, 'What am I going to tell the woman I gave my word to?'"

"What reason did your father give for rejecting the proposal?"

"That it had come from a city boy. My father claimed he could get a more appropriate match from his village."

"That's all? Do people still abide by such stereotypes?"

"They do. They push you to marry someone 'from home.' But in this case, it was no more than a pretext. Father had married a pair of city girls himself. He had other motives, as you'll soon see. He arranged the match, and we had to go down to Marrakech."

"So you went?"

"Yes I went. Full of reservations, and crying the whole way, but I went."

"You submitted without a fight?"

"I complied. Compliance is a little different from submission. I considered the whole thing a farce, completely arbitrary, but that didn't spare me the grief of shock. The farce was happening to me. All the way there I kept seeing omens along the road; a jack-knifed truck, a bird smacking the windshield, a dead dog, a black dead dog in the middle of the road. Even the weather turned ominous. It was mid July, but the sky filled abruptly with dark clouds that lay against the horizon like some awful, angry giant.

"The car started playing up too, as if someone or something was holding it back. Then came the storm. A wall of rain slapped the car and we couldn't see a thing. We had to stop. It was eerie, unnatural. My mother at some gas station in the middle of nowhere, tense, reciting the Qur'an and fingering her rosary: *A'uzu billah min ash-shaytan al-rajim, bismillah al-rahman al-rahim.* I will never forget it.

"That night I had a dream. I saw a woman swaying in pain, stumbling through a barren thorny scrubland. As she approached, I could see that her throat had been cut. I woke with my hand to my own throat, feeling the same pain.

"But when I met the family, the load on my chest lifted. I felt suddenly at ease. I felt a keen desire to get on with things. How do you explain that?"

"From some of the stories I've already been told, I suspect you'll tell me it was something supernatural."

"Yes, it was witchcraft. Sorcery. Of course, I didn't know that at the time. During that visit I fell in love with the man, deeply in love, before I'd even seen him. We went back to Rabat and I could think of nothing but him. Moroccans are accomplished sorcerers, my dear. Or sorceresses. We cause miscarriages, make men impotent, turn girls into spinsters, tear husbands from their wives. Meanwhile, we talk about our 'peaceful society' and delude ourselves that violence is a foreign disease. Because our violence can happen without guns or bloodshed, it's beyond the law. Why would I try to hide it from you who might know us better than we know ourselves?"

"It obviously unsettles you."

"Why wouldn't it? I was directly affected. It's not a matter of hearing someone else's stories. No matter how well death is described, who can conceive the event itself, never having died? Yet, I think every Moroccan, knows what it's like to be killed by a spell. Education, rank, class, none of them makes you immune. But try getting people to talk about it. It's taboo.

"I saw an interview in the paper with Nizar Qabbani, the great Syrian poet. The journalist was accusing him of some political indiscretion, I can't remember what exactly. But Qabbani lost his temper and said, 'What Moroccan magician gave you that?' It's probably a popular saying in the Near East."

"Well," said my American. "You know it's in your history.

Morocco has always had a reputation for state of the art sorcery."

I started laughing and couldn't stop. "When things get bad enough, the only thing to do is laugh," I said. "It's a saying of ours."

"What did I say that made you laugh so much?" asked Susan.

"It's that term 'state of the art.' It's as if you were talking about the weapons technology in your own country. I reckon we Moroccans have got a state of the art defense system, after all."

"I wasn't making fun. I have to call it something."

"I'd call it ignorance. Ignorance in general and ignorance of Islam. The persistence of sorcery proves that paganism is not dead. But then, I don't know. Don't think I have the answers to all of your questions."

"Let's get back to your story."

"Yes. This was man number five. He was studying in France at the time. We went to see his family, and very soon afterwards he forgot about his exams and came to Rabat to see me. He lived in a hotel."

"You're kidding. And you attribute that behaviour to witchcraft?"

"It's obvious."

"How do they do it?"

"I don't know. I don't want to know. Later he went back to France, but this time I followed him."

"Go on!"

"During the flight I felt I wanted to jump out and get there before the plane landed. I felt an irresistible, an inexplicable craving to be on French soil."

"Go on."

"It was all much more complicated on his side. He had a French fiancée, and his family was using me, using his engagement to me, to make him break off the other relationship. They were using witchcraft to do it. But the story's hardly begun. There were intrigues within intrigues within intrigues."

"How so?"

"Well. Evidently the plan had worked too efficiently. He broke off his engagement with the French girl and was going to come back to Morocco to finalize the marriage contract with me. Then his family began to hesitate, now that the fiancée was out of the picture. They started using witchcraft again, this time to break our relationship, so that their boy could get his degree. Believe it or not. Many wouldn't. I wouldn't believe it myself, if I hadn't been there."

"Why should I not believe you? Morocco isn't the only place in the world where people have turned to witchcraft. We have it in parts of the States, and we had it in the past. You've probably heard of the Salem Witch Trials. I'm sure you know how witches were burned in medieval Europe."

"You were more advanced than we are, even in your Middle Ages," I said. "We are living our Middle Ages now, at least by the Islamic calendar, but we don't burn our witches."

"I appreciate your outspokenness."

"Not as much as I appreciate the opportunity to talk. Do you think a Moroccan would ask these kinds of questions? And we don't go to psychoanalysts, either."

"At least you don't have their outrageous bills to worry about."

"The plane finally landed, and he met me at the airport in Paris. He was wearing dark glasses to hide a black eye he had got in some casino. He claimed he had been hit by a soccer ball and I claimed to believe it. In time I learned the truth, and not just about his chronic gambling. There was also the French fiancée, the witchcraft, his bouts of heavy drinking. Everything came out in the end, including my father's hand in the whole affair."

"Your father knew all along?"

"Yes. And once it became clear that I knew he had known, he started objecting to the match for form's sake. He started saying that the boy was a gambler and a drunk, that the sister was a witch and a whore. But he had known all this from the start. He'd set the whole thing up as a way of getting rid of the civil servant who'd gone so far as to come to our house and propose marriage. The match had been a farce from day one. My father had known it, the boy's sister had known it, I suspected it, yet we all went on playing our roles."

"What about the boy? Surely he must have known too."

"He did, but he got so involved with me that the idea of

completing the marriage became an obsession with him. He insisted that his family finalize a marriage contract with me in writing, as soon as possible. We would live together as man and wife after his graduation. We finally got the contract written up. And then he was dragged to Morocco by what amounted to a military decree."

"A military decree?"

"He had received a grant from the army to do veterinary studies. His sister had him suddenly recalled to Morocco. She had connections with important officers remember, intimate connections. So he came back, and stayed just long enough for the sister to pull him in front of two notaries and ask to have the contract annulled. He was back on a plane to France within twenty-four hours. It happened as fast as one of those old-fashioned eviction notices, when the mayor of a village would send his goons around to drag people screaming from their houses."

"He agreed to this?"

"He had no say in the matter. And his sister had connections with all the right people, if not the devil himself."

"But how did it come to this. Why the back-stabbing?"

"Just my luck, I guess. The witch owned her brother. She had paid for him. Some people simply can't stand to see love happen. Call it narcissism, jealousy, a compulsion to meddle in the affairs and fortunes of others. I'm no psychoanalyst, but I know a sick obsession when I see one. People like that woman are so full of spite they will stop at nothing to choke love before it grows."

"Was she that bad?"

"I've said what I think."

"I hardly know what to think. It's too strange."

"That woman hated me before she'd even met me. I could have been anyone; she'd have felt just the same way. I'd like to know what your feminists, with all their prattle about 'sisterhood,' would make of it. You know, the most insidious plot I've encountered in my life, was carried out against me by a girlfriend at school, the only other girl in the class. She did her best to see that I failed the final exams. If woman has an enemy, it's other women. Even a husband who betrays his wife uses another woman to do it. Some even use their wives' sisters to do it. Is that the sisterhood you talk about?"

"Isn't it possible that your fiancé's sister had some reason to hate you? Perhaps you said something."

"I only met her three times. When they proposed marriage, when the contract was drawn up and once when she invited us to her house. That was the day we saw her for what she was."

"Why would someone who hated you so intensely invite you to her house?"

"I'll tell you why. That evening while the house was alive with music and dancing, someone was in the garage dismantling my car. They took off a door panel, and stuffed the space behind it full of witchery."

"To obstruct the marriage?"

"All I know is that I left her house swearing I wouldn't marry her brother if he were the last man on earth. Even my mother, who had wanted the marriage to go ahead, picked it up. 'I'd rather you stayed single,' she said in the car on the way home. 'That man may be a flower, but he's growing from a garbage heap.' We didn't know about the stuff behind the door until the panel fell off seven years later. It was horrible! It's horrible to think what some women are capable of. They're the kind who would cut their last tie to God, as my mother would say."

"So all your years of waiting led to nothing."

"The pain of waiting is like the pain of death. It's a pain no one can conceive until it's upon them. I began to associate my experience with a movie I'd seen, a movie that summed up my feelings exactly and which took on a new and unbearable significance because of it. It's the story of a woman who loves some fugitive from justice. She waits until all that's left for her is the hell of waiting."

"The same hell you were in?"

"I measured days like a prisoner. Once the doorbell rang in the middle of the night. I woke in terror and went to the door to ask who was there. 'Aisha!' came my fiancé's voice. 'Aisha, it's me! Open up!' I opened and there was nothing but wind and night. Don't tell me it was a hallucination."

"No. It sounds like something from a Brontë novel."

"Or a fairy tale."

"And you still believe the charms of a sorceress were enough to wreck your relationship?"

"Listen to this. It's from the Qur'an: *But they learned from the two angels how they might separate a man from his wife . . . .* No one can have the feeling I have for this verse. I know exactly what it means. I understand it with my blood."

"Is that the whole passage?"

"No. Here it is: *They follow the council of Satan in the reign of Solomon. And Solomon blasphemed not, but Satan blasphemed, teaching the people magic. And they follow also what was sent down unto the two angels in Babel, Harut, and Marut. To none did the two teach it, until they had said: 'We are but a temptation, so blaspheme not.' But they learned from the two angels how they might separate a man from his wife, though they could harm none thereby save by the will of God. But the people preferred to learn what is harmful and does not profit them. Assuredly they knew that whoso traffics in magic, has no portion in the Hereafter. And surely vile is the price for which they have bartered themselves, would that they knew!*"

"Thank you. What finally happened to your fiancé?"

"Nothing. He went back to the void he had come from. I forgot everything, his features, every little detail . . . . It was all wiped clean like sand on a beach, wiped out with one touch of the waves. Yet if I talked about it, I cried like a child. I don't know how to describe it. The process was far from gentle. It was a crude amputation that left a jagged scar."

"You describe it well."

"The backbone of our literature is poetry. The miracle of our religion is the Qur'an."

"You're here now, speaking coherently, without tears."

"Yes. I have gradually come back to myself. Time can heal the most savage wounds."

"Neither your father nor the man's sister will ever realize what harm they did the two of you."

"Nor the magnitude of their sin."

"I'm surprised that a man with the sort of faults you describe in your fiancé would have prompted such deep feelings in you."

"Love has little to do with reason. He had his faults, all right, but he also behaved with perfect grace and refinement, he had learned the best France has to offer. Whether we were alone or in company, in a restaurant, even when he was apologizing, you couldn't help but love him."

"I remember," said Susan, "when the BBC was doing a series in which an elderly woman returns home to her brother one evening, and he's alarmed because she seems very disoriented. 'Where have you been?' he asks. 'To the movies.' 'What did you see?' 'A man and a woman.' 'Seeing a man and a woman has done all this?' 'Well,' she explains, 'it's a *French*man and a woman.'"

My American laughed at her story then added seriously, "It is cross-culturalism. Your fiancé had spent a good deal of time with his French friend, and had genuinely adopted what you call French grace and refinement, as his own."

"What makes you think so?"

"Because he appealed to your mother. Didn't you say she called him a flower? Even if he was a flower, he was growing from a heap of garbage. I would really like to know her side of the story to bring in a new voice and perspective. Could we arrange an interview with her? I'd be so grateful. You could sit in if you like, but you wouldn't have to translate. I should be able to handle it with my Arabic."

So it was that Susan the American researcher came back to the house another day, and I heard the tragedy from my mother's angle.

My mother poured tea and extended a glass to our guest.

"May we drink it at Aisha's wedding," she remarked as she took the glass; a clever, idiomatic expression that broke the ice perfectly.

"I'm not so sure we can, *lal* . . . ." My mother was about to say *lalla*, but caught herself in time. What could she call the foreigner? Daughter? Dear? Neither were appropriate. Our vernacular is tightly cut to fit very specific social and religious contexts.

"Susan," I intervened. "Call her Susan. I thought I'd told you her name."

"I'm not so sure, Susan," my mother continued, "about drinking tea at Aisha's wedding. They won't allow it. God knows we tried, but they wouldn't let it happen. That woman came to us of her own choice, and it turned out she was manipulating us all along. I know Aisha's told you about her. She invited us all the way to Marrakech. That was the longest evening of my life. The house was full of military big-shots dancing with women. The woman's own daughter wiggling around on a tabletop, right in front of her father. Just fourteen years old!

"There was a blind singer there with his band. She told him to sing a song about the Prophet, and he refused. 'I won't do it,' he said. 'not when I'm drunk.' At least he had some dignity left. Better than the rest. There were women there with their caftans open to the thigh. It was awful. The place was full of high-ranking officers, and she had them twisted around her finger, as she did her own family. Even her mother was terrified of her.

"It wasn't natural. I'm not one to gossip, but the woman was a witch. She told a story that night about how her driver had been five minutes late to pick her up at the hammam. 'What time did I ask you to come?' she asked the driver. 'Five.' 'What time is it now?' 'Five after.' 'You are late.' 'What's five minutes?' the man said, little suspecting what those words would cost.

"The woman bypassed her own husband at his office and asked to speak to his boss. She told the boss to lock the driver up for a few days, then send him back to her. Well, when she told me that, I asked her if she wasn't afraid the driver would hurt her, or try to get his revenge in some way.

You should have heard her. 'Hurt me? How could he hurt me? He came back like a dog. He knew my power.' Those were her very words. I knew the marriage would never work. The day they asked for Aisha's hand I had a dream. I saw a beautiful house with a safe full of money. There was an older man there, slightly bald. He was playing in the garden with some children and I heard a voice say, 'This is Aisha's house. And this is her husband.'"

"She sounds evil enough!" said Susan.

"She was evil. She got her oldest brother to marry an orphan girl, then forced the poor thing to work as her maid. After the girl had given birth to five boys, she called in two notaries to have them draw up the girl's repudiation without even informing her brother. The notaries, to their credit, said they couldn't do it without the husband's consent. So they went to the brother, and he said he had no intention of repudiating anybody, and the notaries cursed the witch and high-tailed it out of there."

"It's a blessing that Aisha never married into such a family."

"May God punish her, and all who hurt women. The brother Aisha was going to marry had been living with a foreign woman for years. That's why she came for my daughter's hand in the first place. She wanted to get at the foreigner by using my daughter. May she be struck with blindness. The foreign woman found out about Aisha and immediately got pregnant."

"To force the brother to marry her, you mean?"

"That's right. But he couldn't do it. His sister was too powerful, she controlled him. The French girl didn't know about that. May God protect our daughters, and the daughters of Muslims from such affliction. He was here on holiday when the witch told him he could go ahead and send for the French girl, and marry her if he wanted to. She came by boat and they met her in Tangier."

"And then?"

"What happened then is unbelievable, but I heard it from a reliable source who saw the whole thing. The French girl had no sooner gotten off the boat, than she started saying she couldn't stand the sight of her lover any more. She'd been bewitched, pure and simple. Hadn't she traveled all that way to get married? Wasn't she pregnant with the man's child? How could she feel such hatred all of a sudden, if not for a spell?"

I sat taking it all in. I hadn't known my mother had kept track of the story, and never would have done, if not for the American's Ph.D. dissertation. And yet, I listened impassively, as if this story were about people I didn't know. I felt indifferent, even when my mother's account reached its climax.

"Then one day Aisha's father came to me and said he had some news, but that I shouldn't tell Aisha. 'What news?' I said. 'The guy's still in France,' he said. 'He's in jail.' God knows what that was about. Maybe the French girl had sued him for child support. In any case, he served his sentence, and they kicked him out of the country. That's the story! The witch finished her brother off for good. He didn't get married and he didn't finish school either. I told Aisha's father, 'It's God's punishment for what they did to my daughter. The worst is still to come. Wait and see.' And he said, 'You don't have to act so pleased about it.' As if he were some impeccable Muslim. Some men are disgusting. Ours, I mean. Not yours."

"How about some women?"

"They're disgusting too. At least yours don't practice sorcery."

Several months went by. I received a small package from Susan that contained the cassette of our interview, and this note:

Dear Aisha,

I went back to transcribe our interview, only to find the cassette scrambled. I had tested it before, and it was working fine. I always check the cassettes. It's the first thing they teach us at school. Why was it working then, and not now? The other interviews are all OK. Why would yours have gone haywire all of a sudden? I cannot think of a technical explanation. But I certainly am upset at the loss of time, and especially at the loss of a document that meant so much to my project.

I do not understand this or maybe, I am afraid, I do. As you said yourself, some things cannot be explained rationally, some things are beyond belief.

Thank you anyway, and please give my regards to your mother.

Susan

Philadelphia, 28 September 1990

I put the tape in my machine. The sounds that came out were as tangled and disturbing as the stuff we had pulled from the door of my car twenty years before.

4

My days in administration shot past, like images seen from an express train window. Our boss managed to keep his hands off public funds and his female employees. He may have been tempted, but if so, he never yielded. He had a scientific and pragmatic mind, and the kind of integrity one does not encouter every day.

Prevailing wisdom decreed that to be democratic with workers in Morocco was pointless. Everyone said you had to treat Moroccan employees like dirt, otherwise they would interpret your behavior as a sign of weakness and grow slack. Our boss ran counter to that notion. He proved that Moroccans too will respect a friendly boss if that boss is competent and has a strong personality.

He taught me that two brains are better than one, and three better than two, regardless of difference in rank. The boss, the typist, the driver and the office boy, each is an equally vital link in getting the work done, each important in a unique way. At the same time, no one should be able to regard himself as indispensable. "Receive anyone who comes with a grievance. Listen to them, even if that's all you can do," our boss used to tell us. "Let them pour it all out."

But somehow, my colleagues always seemed to slip away and I ended up doing the listening on my own. I heard everyone and everything under the sun. There was the man whose neighbor's pipes drained into his house, the wife whose husband had run off and left her without so much as a stitch of clothing to wear, the guy whose colleague was making use of the ministry phone to set up romantic trysts; someone who wanted a taxi license, another from the Sahara who wanted a plane permit.

Once an old Berber from down South came into the office, sat down and wiped his shaved pate with a handkerchief. "My neighbor . . . ," he said at last. "My neighbor is a socialist. He's in the opposition party. When the government news comes on the radio, he tells his son, 'Turn that crap off, will you?'"

That was it. He had come six hundred kilometers on a third class bus to tell me that. I did not mind letting people 'pour it all out,' but this was absurd.

Another time, a northerner burst into the office, angry and tense. He started complaining about some policeman who had deliberately tossed all his belongings into the street. "It that fair?" he asked me bitterly.

I sent inquiries and it was not long before a second man came in with a different version. He said that the 'victim' had been living across the street from him in a shack. He was dirt-poor and had half a dozen children, so the man, moved by pity and a sense of religious duty, had invited his impoverished neighbor and his family into his house, as there was a vacant room downstairs.

"So, they moved out of their miserable shack and into my house. One day my wife is using the mortar and pestle, and this guy grabs a stick and starts banging the ceiling. 'What in the world are you doing?' my wife called down. 'What're *you* doing?' the man shouted. When I came home the guy was screaming his head off at my wife, and when I heard what it was about, I told him to get out of my house at once. He refused and I called a policeman who came and threw the guy's stuff out into the street.

"I was just trying to be a good neighbor. He was fine at first, but it didn't take him long to show his true colors. I didn't have much choice but to go for the police. It was nine at night, and the guy was standing out in the street with his family and all his stuff, calling for help, saying he won't leave, that it's his right to stay, as if he were paying me rent or something."

"Do you own the house?" I asked.

"No, I rent it for three hundred dirhams a month. It has running water now. It didn't when I moved in. I installed electricity too. Just getting water cost me six thousand dirhams. All together I paid ten thousand dirhams to fix it up. It is right on the main avenue. If you're ever in town, you're bound to drive right past it. Just go beyond the mosque and you'll see a mechanic's, you can't miss it. The house is the next building on your left."

"Go on!" I thought, somewhat sardonically. "Take your time, pour it all out! I am here to listen."

He explained that he had come to Rabat for a religious meeting and had taken the opportunity to come and explain his position. "I'm an Idrissi *sherif*," he added. "Look at this." He produced an ancient looking piece of parchment, carefully wrapped and stowed in his satchel. "See here," he said, smoothing the document on my desk. "It's got the royal stamp of Sultan Moulai 'Abd al-'Aziz and the Islamic date right here." He insisted I visit him if I ever happened to be near his village.

I thought the visit would end there, but the *sherif* was enjoying his seat and the opportunity to chat, and started telling me about how plowing had started, and how green the land was turning after the last rains, and how too much sun was not good because ants would come and steal the seeds, and several hundred other things.

"I can't believe the cost of living in Rabat," he said. "It's a blessing God made vegetables the way He did, so that they won't keep. Otherwise, people would store them up and speculate on the price. But God in His wisdom knows best. Either you sell vegetables at the market price or they rot." And so he went on, ending at last with a prediction of prosperity for the village thanks to a new set of irrigation channels.

Once, an anonymous letter came in that read:

Tangier, 30 October 1989
Dear Sirs,
I am writing to you in connection with the words of our Prophet: "Whoever of you witnesses abomination must change it with deeds and if he cannot, then with words, and if not then, by opposing it with his heart, the latter being the weakest degree of faith."

The French Mission in Tangier is teaching Muslim children a book about our lord Muhammad, God's prayer and peace be upon him, written by a Jew who alleges that the message revealed to our Prophet was mere hallucination.

I am including a copy of that book to fulfill my duty, even though my action represents but the lowest form of faith. I leave it to you, who are in a position of authority to deal with this abomination.

A concerned Muslim.

This letter was raised at a meeting where one of our number, a certain Benabdallah, dismissed it saying, "It's not worth discussing. This is a question of freedom of speech and we needn't interfere." Not worth discussing? Freedom of speech? When our children's minds were being cast into doubt about their religion? And what does it mean that this man's name evokes *Allah*? He got off without so much as a reprimand. He probably was not even sober when he said it.

Benabdallah had been appointed to his position on the strength of a business card belonging to some influential personage. The card implied, "Give him a promotion," and they did, from the position of supply manager to senior manager. From distributing pencils and cleaning products to making decisions. Ignorance and good intentions had combined to produce yet another senior manager of chaos. Our Prophet was right: "When responsibility is entrusted to those who cannot bear it, expect the apocalypse."

Benabdallah always kept that business card close at hand, in the breast pocket of his jacket. He'd fish it out between two fingers and hold it up, oblivious to the glances being exchanged around him, and say, "Look who's backing Benabdallah!"

"Why don't you have that card plastic-coated?" I once suggested. "You'll wear it out if you don't."

"Perhaps I will," he replied, deflecting the irony, well aware of my opinion of him. He came to me a little later, out of the blue and said, "Why don't you take me seriously? I'm a manager too, you know. Who do you think you are?"

Benabdallah had proved what he was on my very first day at work. I had not been in my new office half an hour when a note arrived: "There's a file I need to go over with you. I'll be in the office on Saturday afternoon at three o'clock." What sort of file do a Moroccan man and a Moroccan woman examine together in an empty office building on a Saturday afternoon, I ask you? But that was the best his limited imagination could produce. As if we are so devoted to work that we dedicate our weekends.

When I saw him on the Monday, he threw me a cutting glance. The poor thing had waited all Saturday afternoon. It did not take long for him to exact his revenge. I came in one morning to find my office empty, save for a phone in the middle of the floor.

"What happened to my furniture?" I asked the office boy.

"That's life for you, my girl!" he replied sympathetically. (The office 'boy' was in fact an old man.) "Benabdallah ordered it moved to the office of some new person they've just hired."

I went to the director and threw a fit. He called in Benabdallah.

"Why didn't you get my permission before you moved her things?" he demanded.

"Well, I . . . ," Benabdallah stammered. "I didn't think she needed that office all to herself. I thought she could move in with the typists."

"You get that furniture back where it belongs!" Benabdallah left with his tail between his legs.

On one occasion we were in a meeting discussing a piece of land that had been donated as the site for a new center for abandoned children. Benabdallah's fat hand went up, with its ostentatious block of gold ring, his belly wedged between chair and table. When he opened his mouth, the room stank with the liquor he had spent half the night drinking.

"Give it back to 'em," he slurred. "We don't want their land. It's out in the middle of nowhere. There's nothing out there, no monuments, nothing. There's nobody famous from there. We wouldn't even know who to name the center after."

The room filled with an embarrassed silence. Even the director was lost for words. The incident was eventually filed away in the collection we referred to as "Benabdallah's precious utterances."

When there was talk about a government reshuffle, rumour got about that Benabdallah was having himself fitted out for a national costume with the expectation of being officially appointed as a minister. He was sitting by the phone, waiting for the call. When the new appointment was announced, Benabdallah stopped coming to work in protest, but instead of a reprimand, he got a promotion to director; a conciliatory gesture.

Benabdallah was now my boss. He inaugurated the new era by settling his old score with me. I was no longer included in meetings, and was given nothing even moderately compelling to do; the old tactic of forcing someone to resign by sidelining them.

Back in the days when Benabdallah was still head of supplies, he had given the office boy a huge box one afternoon and said, "Put this in the trunk of my car. It's unlocked. You know the one, it's the blue Fiat 127." The box contained everything from soap to brooms, all destined for Benabdallah's home. But somehow the boy put the box in the blue Fiat 127 of another employee.

It did not take much imagination to guess what had happened. the employee came back the next morning gleefully telling anyone who would listen about the box he had found in his trunk, and just as gleefully imagining the look that had been on Benabdallah's face when he had not found the box in his. Someone suggested we write to the *Islamic Advisor*, a religious program on TV, and ask whether it was permissible to steal from a thief. "Or if it's permitted to steal public property," someone else retorted, but it was decided that the *Islamic Advisor* would not touch such a 'political' question.

I myself used to find Benabdallah in the supply room, on the phone taking notes from his wife. Then he would call her sister in the Sahara, give her his wife's message, and take down a new one. He would be saying, "She wants green and red . . . . No, it has to be wool. How much per ball?" Then he would hang up and call his wife: "Ten dirhams a ball. Do you want it?" Then back to the sister: "She'll take twenty of each." Finally he took to calling his wife on one phone, and her sister on the other, and letting them deal directly, receiver to receiver.

Benabdallah's nerve knew no bounds. His brother-in-law had a phone at home but used to come to our office to make long-distance calls, Benabdallah standing magnanimously by, as if he were paying from his own pocket.

"Do you know anyone overseas?" he asked me once. "Because if you do, I can get you the director's internatonal line. He's out of town, you know, and his secretary won't mind. She's nice."

"No." I said "I don't need to call anyone overseas."

"OK, fine, but would you mind making a call for me in English? I've been wanting to get in touch with this Pakistani guy I met on the *hajj*. Come on, help me out!" And yet he had the gall to harp on sanctimoniously about the "fat-cats" who defrauded millions from public funds.

"The small fry steals from public funds too, you know," I reminded him. "When someone takes home a bar of soap, for instance . . . or toilet paper, or rugs, for example, what would you call that? What about people who use a ministry phone to make personal calls, or to let their family make personal calls? If each employee took home just one pen and a sheet of paper, don't you realize what it would cost the treasury?"

But he really did not see anything wrong in it. The administration was not a person, after all. You were not taking anything from anyone in particular. Benabdallah registered my not-very-subtle insinuations and kept quiet, but a few days later he came to me in private, a bold smile on his lips.

"The other day you were telling me about people who steal public funds by making personal calls and taking home pens."

"And toilet paper and rugs."

"OK! OK! I want to tell you something right now. This administration steals and cheats and deprives me of my rights and you of yours too. At least I'm smart enough to get something back. Why shouldn't I?" A classic case of the wrongdoer justifying his actions in order to be at peace with himself.

By the time Benabdallah became my boss I had built up a horrible record with him.

"I'd be better off staying at home," I told my family, thinking it was time to throw in the towel.

"He'll forget," they said.

"Not likely," I replied, but then I changed my tack a little. "Whether he forgets or not isn't really the point. It's better to quit than to sit around that office all day doing nothing."

"You're crazy," my mother retorted. "That's just what he wants you to do. Do you want to help him get what he wants? Do you think getting a job is easy? Look around you. Look at all the unemployment, even among people with degrees. He doesn't own the ministry, he can't hold a position he's not entitled to forever. Just be patient."

One of the first changes that people noticed after Benabdallah's promotion, was in his secretary. Her dresses got shorter and were cut lower, front and back, and sometimes one would see her with the phone in one hand, a cigarette in the other and two bare feet propped on the desk. One colleague saw her enter Benabdallah's office, reach into his jacket pocket and remove a few bills from his wallet in front of a somewhat startled visitor.

Benabdallah's first official signature in his new position gave that secretary a glorified new title and a fat salary to go with it. She was only a typist and receptionist for all that, though she presumably had 'other duties.' Benabdallah started taking her on all his business trips, and she would come back glowing with talk of high class hotels, fancy villas, limousine rides, wonderful gifts . . . .

As for Benabdallah himself, he too started singing a new tune: "Whoever says Morocco isn't making progress is trying to block the sun with a sieve. Today's Morocco has nothing to do with the Morocco of the past. Ask the international organizations. They'll tell you that Morocco can no longer be classified a third-world country."

When I heard about all that, I had this to say: "But that doesn't keep one from wishing for a little more progress, does it? And it isn't going to happen as long as incompetent people hold positions of responsibility. It isn't going to happen when those positions are handed out like candy through corrupt middlemen!" Benabdallah stiffened and averted his eyes.

"Corruption is hardly a Moroccan specialty," he said. "It's everywhere."

"That doesn't make it right."

"You never get it, do you?" he snapped. "Who do you think you are, anyway?"

Who did I think I was? He had obviously not forgotten his Saturday afternoon at the office. "It will take more than hired cars and hotel suites to make your kind feel secure," I thought. He stopped little short of demanding to know why I wouldn't respect him—he was my boss after all—justifying a position he had bought with his connections. Had it not been for that business card, he would still have been stealing brooms.

One of my colleagues had taken maternity leave and not come back, even though the baby was nine months old. At last someone complained, and the woman received a notice signed by none other than Benabdallah. When she went in to see him about it, a secretary friend of mine was there to witness his fawning apology. He slapped his forehead and said, "I'm sorry! I signed that paper without thinking. I didn't realize you were Mouddin's wife. My apologies to you both. Go home and stay as long as you like. If there's something for you to do I'll send it along with your husband. At least you're raising a family, not like that slut who turned you in!"

That same secretary used to tell how she would go in and find Benabdallah asleep at his desk. Once he woke up and said, "These chairs are comfortable. One can't help dozing off."

"I'm sure you've got nothing better to do," she burst out, and then hearing her own words she added quickly, "I mean, I'm sure you've done all your work and deserve a rest."

Our ministry was reputed to be haunted. The night watchman reported having seen lights in Benabdallah's office late one night and that when he had gone to investigate he had found a ghost sitting at the desk reading a paper. Later Benabdallah called a meeting to announce a supernatural encounter of his own.

He opened the meeting with those words. "What're you trying to do, scare me to death? How often do I have to tell you to turn off the lights? Last night, I had to go by Bilqadi's office because they'd been left on. I reached for the switch and a voice called out, 'Don't do it!' so I reached a second time and it happened again. It was Bilqadi's voice. I almost had a heart attack."

Benabdallah's stupidity was legendary. Once he was asked a sensitive question at an important meeting. He didn't have a clue how to answer, so he got up, left the room and found out what he needed to know from one of his employees. Unfortunately, he forgot it on the way back to the meeting.

"It was so embarrassing," said the man who had reported the incident.

"What did he do?" someone asked.

"Just sat there. What else could he do?"

"It serves him right! He ought to know that he's out of his depth by now."

It was around that time that Benabdallah started talking about finding another job.

"It's getting to be too much for me," he said with a sigh. "Time to let some young blood take over."

"And what will you do?"

"I'll do what that guy Himi did, start up a catering service. You know, rent out chairs and pots. Himi started with a few glasses. Look where he is today."

Eventually, a group of typists came to me to complain. Things were getting out of hand.

"Everyone has had it up to here," they said. "The old director was a fair man. He went by the rules. We were all treated equally and we accepted things, but not anymore. Not when we see people promoted from out of nowhere. Not when we've worked hard for a promotion only to have to sit and watch as someone is moved up just to get in on free gas and the use of a car."

I left them sitting in my office, and went straight to Benabdallah's. I entered without knocking and spoke before he had a chance.

"There's a group of typists in my office, right now, representing the staff here. They're talking about arbitrary promotions and a general disregard for the rules, and they're mad as hornets. Everyone, from the drivers to the swithchboard operators is ready for their magic promotion too."

Benabdallah stared at me, flustered, then lowered his

head. His hands fidgeted and his voice trembled; he said he had the right to do as he wished, and started on about his prerogatives and how he played by the rules."

I went back to the office and told the hornets that I had delievered their message. Then I wrote my letter:

Rabat, 1 January, 1990
Subject: Resignation
To: The Director,
Further to the discussion I had with you today, and because I feel that it is a crime for me to stay in a job where I do nothing, I am writing to give notice of my resignation. I should have made this decision a year ago [i.e., when you took charge], but I was clinging to certain illusions [i.e., that you would be removed from your post].

May God have mercy on this country and guide it safely through this difficult stage of its life. I trust He is capable of all things.
Aisha Abu al-'Azm

I handed the letter to an office boy and walked out. That was the end of my career, but Benabdallah's had only just begun. He ended up as a minister. What he had not been able to get by pulling strings he got through the democratic process and another wonder of wonders was launched.

His ministry managed to run itself for two years. Then word got out that Benabdallah had been booted out of the

the office, but was still drawing his salary, plus benefits.

One day I met a girl on the street who had been a switchboard operator when I was at the ministry. She told me that when they had changed Benabdallah's carpet they had found underneath it an arsenal of amulets.

"Well," I observed "that explains how he got his position, because it certainly wasn't for his education or ability."

The girl started to tell me about a man she knew who was using spells to get elected to parliament.

"Is he that desperate for money?" I inquired.

"No," she said. "He's loaded. It's a question of prestige."

And what of Benabdallah's secretary? She retained her post and is busy directing her charms towards a new boss.

He came in holding a fancy envelope. A dark young man with an afro, wearing jeans, a white T-shirt and Greek sandals. He handed me the envelope and I invited him to sit down. It was a letter of introduction in appalling French. Irritated, I set it aside and, forcing a smile, said, "So you know Isabelle then?"

"I met her at one of the camps in Tindouf. She works with a refugee organization. But I guess you know all that."

"I met Isabelle in Tunisia at a conference connected with the annual women's day celebrations, though I didn't really see what that event had to do with refugees. She was suspicious of everything the Tunisian government has done regarding women, from the abolition of polygamy to the legalization of abortion. Isabelle considered these were merely decrees handed down from the top. But you know how it is with international organizations, they're never satisfied, even if we break our backs to please them.

"At the end of the conference, Isabelle wouldn't even sign the cable to the Tunisian president. She's a bit arrogant as you probably know. She said, 'What?! You expect me to congratulate them for their 'achievements'? I'm supposed to express my 'gratitude and admiration'? No! Thank you! I'm not representing some Third World government here. We're a responsible international organization.'

"One of the Tunisians who organized the event told me how the president of the Tunisian Women's Organization had met Isabelle at a conference in Paris and been impressed by what she had called her open-minded and liberal views. She told me, 'I personally think her views are spiteful, racist, and colonialist.'

"The Jordanian representative there said to Isabelle in Arabic, 'Europeans are ungrateful and disrespectful. You've taken Tunisian hospitality for granted. You don't even notice the things they've done for you.' Isabelle asked me to translate. I made it as inoffensive as I could."

My guest seemed more at ease after this outburst, almost eager to confide in me.

"Our loyalties are swayed by our stomachs," he said.

"A loaf of sugar and bottle of oil are all it takes to win votes. Democracy and hunger don't mix," I said.

"Now democracy and corruption, that's another story," he retorted.

"Well," I said. "Nobody believes they're buying people tons of sugar and oil out of the kindness of their hearts. It's an investment. The voters know what's going on."

"Why don't they simply take the sugar and vote for whoever they want?"

"They tried that," I said. "So then the candidates switched to shoes. They started giving voters one of a pair, telling them they could claim its mate after the elections, providing of course that they brought in evidence that they'd voted the right way."

"Are you always this outspoken?" he asked.

"I believe in self-criticism, for my own good and for the good of my country. And I guess I don't mind demonstrating that we have some freedom here to say what we think, contrary to what the Polisario's no doubt been telling you. So, then you're one of the 'misled,' and Isabelle wants me to help you? How can I serve you? It's a national duty after all. You're one of the stray lambs come back to the Moroccan fold. Is there something in particular you'd like to see? I'm at your disposal."

He said he wanted most to visit the beaches, and we agreed on Saturday afternoon.

On the way to our rendezvous I felt inexplicably tense. I pulled up at the entrance to his hotel. He emerged instantly, walking slowly, and got into the car. He produced a packet of cigarettes, lit one, blew smoke through his mouth and said, without irony, "Mind if I smoke?"

I drove around the city walls, along the high bluffs overlooking the river, past the mausoleum where Mohammed V is enshrined, then down to the river where a fleet of small boats lay anchored at its mouth, as if for decoration.

"Ahh, the smell of the sea!" he exclaimed.

"It's true! I forget that I live right on the Atlantic. You can't even see the ocean from my neighborhood."

The Oudaya lay before us, a collection of small whitewashed houses running in tiers uphill, topped off by a minaret, the whole surrounded by thick walls. I slowed down to let him look.

"Like a postcard," he said.

"Or a miniature, tempting you to touch it. That's the Oudaya, the Kasbah."

"Kasbah?"

"It means reed."

"How's that?"

"You know, that hollow, stem-like plant, a reed."

"Just because I'm from the Sahara doesn't mean I don't know what a reed is!"

"I wasn't implying that." I smiled. *"The Sahara, land of wealth: sun and sand, a sand softer than silk*. That's from a Moroccan song." He was smiling now, too.

"What does a reed have to do with the Oudaya?" He asked as if addressing a tour guide. Since I didn't know, I answered like a tour guide, saying the first thing that came into my head.

"The word *kasbah*, or reed, was given to walled cities because they were built around springs that had reeds as conduits. That's the general explanation. God knows what the truth is."

We were driving up hill now, close to the walls.

"What're all those holes for?"

The question took me by surprise. I had no idea. Those holes in the walls had always been there and it had never occurred to me to wonder why. As I glanced at them, they lost their familiarity. It was as if I had never seen them before. They were like features in a face being unveiled. The majesty of those walls, with their ancient, sublime gates, moved me to tears. He did not notice.

"Why all the holes?" he demanded again, pulling me back to my role of tour guide.

"They were used to hold scaffolding," I said authoritatively. "Some were plugged, but mostly they just left them. Imagine! Thousands of holes! It seems like a defect, but it gives the walls character, after all. It's part of what they are, works of art. Those walls were built for a practical purpose, but they've ended up as works of art. Out here it's all traffic, noise, and exhaust fumes. In there it's another world, thanks to the walls."

"*A high wall was set between them, in which is a door. Within is mercy, without lies torment.*" He recited the Qur'anic verse and said, "What else is behind those walls?"

"There's one dead-end street, a mosque, a public oven, a cafe, a garden with a fish pond and orange, lemon, fig and olive trees, a palace with courtyard and fountain. Cats lying in the sun."

"It sounds lovely. What a gift to the people of Rabat!"

"Make that to the tourists. I haven't seen the place since I was a child. Like the ocean, we forget it's there."

This was not quite true. I had been to the Oudaya only the month before, taking a break in the garden because the shops across the road, in the old medina were still closed. The flower and herb beds were in bloom, the trees in full-leaf. I took a seat in the sun on a low wall, and basked in the sounds of children's voices, the exuberance of the birds, a dove's sad cry, all set in silence.

A peace came over me, but it was short-lived. A small girl ran past, stumbled, dropped the plastic water bottle she was carrying, and knelt to pick it up. A skinny woman in a thick *djellaba* caught up with her and slapped her hard across the face with a scowl and a curse. It's not just fathers who bring their children up with an iron fist. The girl went off holding her face, followed by the mother. A wet patch was left behind, spreading over the cobbled walk.

That memory depressed me. But I always feel depressed when I drive by the Oudaya walls and down the steep slope between the cemetery and the sea. There, where river meets sea, where city meets cemetery, where the road runs down, an inevitable, sad sense of departure comes over me.

"The sea!" exclaimed my Saharan visitor, as if he had never seen it before. Now I was driving along a stretch of the coast road for the first time in ten years. The sea was magnificent. The beaches had changed so much that I could not recognize them. Resorts had sprung up everywhere. Even the road had changed, and I managed to take a wrong turn somewhere that had us going back towards the city.

It was late summer and the beach where we ended up was deserted, save for a handful of soccer players. The ocean was still and vast. My companion was positioning me with his Japanese camera for a photograph with one of the royal palaces in the background. He pressed the shutter then took a deep breath and stood watching the waves break on the sand.

I ventured a comment on the feeling of peace the sea can bring, perhaps because of its shifting blues, the movement of the water or the perpetual song of the waves. He let out a snort.

"Or the half-naked women!"

His impudence bruised me in my reflections, but I smiled. "I suppose, that would bring peace upon a pure

Arab from the Sahara like yourself. You do claim to be the Arabs, after all."

But his tirade had only just begun.

"Every Moroccan girl you meet insists she's from a respectable family. What about these?" He indicated several girls walking ahead of us in bikinis. "You call this respectability?!"

"The Qur'an warns us not to judge people prematurely, on their appearances. Suspicion of that kind is a sin. Anyway, look at the two of us. Here we are on an empty beach. What conclusions would people jump to about that?"

He was busy watching the girls' backsides. Then he said, as if he had not been listening, "How can you call this a Muslim country?"

"You shouldn't generalize," I said. "You're falling for all the old stereotypes. Don't you realize people here say exactly the same thing about you people from the Sahara?"

"Like what?"

"Like . . . 'How can they call themselves Muslims when they don't fast during Ramadan?' for instance."

"They say that? But the majority of you people who fast don't even pray."

"You Saharans have been filled with misconceptions about us," I said sadly.

"Why is Morocco involved in the Sahara in the first place?" he demanded. I supplied the official explanation, that the Sahara is an integral part of Moroccan territory, but he was not buying it.

"I'll tell you why," he said. "The reasons are economic."

"Why ask me, if you already have the answer? Economic or not, what does it matter so long as it leads to unity in the end. And it will lead to unity, if people let it happen."

"You mean the Polisario?"

"And Qaddafi."

"It's all economics," he insisted.

"It's a goat even if it flies?" I asked. "Do you know that story?"

I could see that he didn't, so I told it: "A Saharan and a man from the uplands were looking at a distant mountain, unable to make out what was standing on the peak. 'It's a goat!' said the Saharan. 'No, it's a bird!' countered the other. This led to an apparently endless dispute, until the non-Saharan said, 'Hold on! Let's wait to see if it flies away. Then we'll know.' 'Even if it flies it's a goat,' concluded the Saharan. What makes you people so stubborn? Camel milk?"

"It's economics," he said again, then added in a teasing tone, "Actually, that peace you feel when you see the sea, it's water."

"This is just like the traveler who noticed how green the country looked when his bus left Tadla and the man sitting next to him waited until they got to Casablanca, three hours later to say, 'That's because of the rain.' Of course it's water. Water is everything. When I saw Monet's water lilies, it brought water to my eyes."

He sat in silence for a long while, then said abruptly, "You look a lot like Maria, and you're intelligent too."

"Maria?" I could not keep the disapproval from my voice.

He grew suddenly awkward and defensive. "She's a secretary I know attached to some human rights organization in the Canaries."

On the way back, the sun was a deep orange disc on the horizon.

"Look at that!" I exclaimed. But he gave only a glance, and looked away, silent and sad. He remarked on the illuminated walls of the palace but otherwise stayed silent for the rest of the journey. At the hotel he shook my hand.

"I'd like to invite you to dinner," he said. "Couscous."

"You're the guest here, not me. Now that I know you want couscous, I'm inviting you."

He went off with the peculiar snatching gait of someone who has grown up in a sea of sand. I drove home with a Gulfi song that had been playing in my mind since I'd heard it that morning still going round my head, complete with its outbreaks of applause, which sounded like water falling.

When he came for dinner, he was holding a large gift. I unwrapped it and was overjoyed to find an excellent reproduction of Monet's Waterlilies. I did not know what to say or how to act. He followed me in to meet the family. Almost at once he was as much at home as if he'd known them all his life, talking freely about the Sahara and answering all their questions.

Saharan women were reputed to be domineering. He

claimed this was due to the hardships of the desert climate, which forced men to treat their women with deference. Women, he said, were naturally cunning and exploited their position. He noted that plumpness, even obesity, were still considered standards of ideal beauty in Saharan women. People deliberately fattened their daughters from childhood. He explained that a truly beautiful woman is one whose backside jiggles three times per step. Then, pointing to me, he said to my mother, "If this daughter of yours were Saharan, she'd never find a husband."

I decided to tell the story about a guy who goes into convulsions whenever he hears the word 'grease.' It was supposed to have happened shortly after Morocco had recovered the territory of the Sahara. On learning that grease was in high demand there, the man invested his every last penny in a truck-load of the stuff, thinking his fortune was made. But when he arrived in the Sahara, no one wanted anything to do with him or his merchandise, and he had to dump the whole lot in the sand. Ever since, the word "grease" has triggered seizures in this man. Or so they said.

We hit all the hot topics, the Sahara issue, fundamentalism, the Gulf war, America and Israel. It was quite late when he looked at his watch and stood to go. I took a last admiring look at his gift. Over my shoulder, he said, "It really is a great painting, worth crying over! I had it sent to me by a friend in Paris."

The whiteness of the open lotus on the dusk-lit surface

of the water was beautiful, his gesture had been beautiful, he was beautiful. I pressed his hand proudly as I walked him to the door. He wanted to speak, hesitated, then in an embarrassed whisper, said, "You're my best friend. I hope you know that."

"I'm your best friend? In Morocco?" I retorted. "That's like hearing you're the most beautiful woman in the whole street."

"And you're demanding too," he grinned. In the hall light, wearing his deep blue jacket, his complexion and eyes seemed darker than ever.

"I'll call you," he said, and walked slowly away up the street. I stood in the doorway and followed him with my eyes. When I turned around, I was face to face with my mother.

"Don't be too hopeful," she said pointedly. "Some Moroccan girl will snap him up, just like that. Marrying Saharan men is popular these days."

I followed her to the kitchen and started washing the dishes. Before long the phone rang.

"Who can that be?" I thought anxiously, and ran to answer.

"Aisha!" His voice.

"Yes! Are you all right?"

"I'm fine."

"It's late? Did you forget something?"

"Well, yes. I forgot to invite you to a concert of classical music tomorrow evening. It's organized by the Goethe Institute. Seven o'clock. Will you come?"

"Yes, thank you. I'd like that."

So again, the next day I found him waiting at his hotel. He climbed into the car and automatically fastened his seat-belt.

"Good evening!" he said.

"God's peace be upon you!" I replied and felt a sudden thrill of joy. His skin had a smoky hue like that of some East Indians. His people were called 'blue men' by the French. It sounded magical. They called themselves 'green men.' Rainbow people, I thought, and smiled. He remarked the smile and misinterpreted it. "I guess I think I'm still in Tenerife," he said, unfastening the seat-belt. "No need to chain ourselves in." The belt snapped back into place.

"So, it looks like your family allowed you to come. Any problems there?"

"I'm not an adolescent, you know. They're used to me working on my own, they have a lot of confidence in me."

He kept silent a long time then said, "Your mother mentioned last night that you're quite religious."

His tone surprised me. It was as if my mother had pointed out some defect in me. He was waiting for a denial. Instead, I confirmed it without hesitation. His silence continued. I sensed disappointment.

We entered the theater where my eyes were drawn to the huge bunch of dahlias spotlighted at the edge of the stage. He looked around him and exclaimed, "Here they come!"

"Who?"

"More of the misled." He laughed, pointing out a group

of young Saharan men who looked more or less like copies of himself, filing down the aisle. I felt nothing as I watched them, and started asking myself what made the man at my side special.

The music began; sounds from another world, making the flowers seem to pulse with energy. He was sitting next to me and something was being woven between us, a lovely tapestry on the loom of a master artist. During the intermission the audience dispersed, and again he had to bring up the question of my religiousness.

"It bothers you, doesn't it?" My eyes were on his. I felt his fascination, as strong as my own.

"Why shouldn't it? Would it be all right for us to meet?"

"Yes!"

"In a café?"

"Be serious. This isn't Madrid."

"In a restaurant?"

"If it's the right kind of restaurant."

"What is this? Moroccans are always claiming that this isn't the third world. Maria says . . . ." He checked himself, looking as if he wished he could press a rewind button and drag the script backwards. I tensed, anxiousness sounding in my voice.

"Maria?"

"I mentioned her before, I think. The secretary I met in the Canaries. That's all." He was embarrassed. Trying to relieve the tension, he added in an exaggerated courtroom tone, "I solemnly swear it, your honor."

"Somehow, I don't trust you under oath; shifty as the desert sands, I'd say."

"Damn you, Aisha." Then he tried to laugh off my insult and his.

"What were you doing in the Canaries in the first place?" I inquired. He claimed he had been a student there, that he had graduated six years before. I scrutinized the gray hair at his temples and said coolly, "You must be quite young then."

"No," he said. "I'm not young."

"At home they refer to you as 'the handsome young man.' 'Your wonderful friend.' They like you," I added, "regardless of the political issue. They like you very much. They often ask me about you and I say, 'I don't see him.'"

That pulled the plug on his smile and he threw me a questioning, disapproving glance.

"Well, I hardly see you."

"I'm in my shell," he said, adding ironically, "too busy with work."

"They're asking me whether all Saharan people look like you and what kind of relationship I have with you."

"They don't all look like me," he replied seriously. "What do you tell them about our relationship?"

"I've told them you were referred to me by a Spanish woman I met in Tunisia; that she asked me to help you until you got your feet on the ground. I told them you're doing fine and don't in fact need me."

"But I do," he smiled. "I can't even get back to my hotel without you."

"Right! You might fall on your face," I said.

"I need your friendship, I really do. You're the best friend I have."

The three-minute bell rang. People went back to their seats, the lights faded, the music resumed, but it was no longer magic. The sharp tone of the violin and its mournful melody grated on my nerves. The dahlias now seemed one dimensional and tastelessly arranged. I felt hot and stifled; his presence made it worse. When it was finally over, I thanked him as we left the auditorium.

"I do like this kind of music," I said, "but I never go to concerts. I don't have friends here really. Most of my friends are abroad."

"You're an intellectual, aren't you? You must know other Moroccan intellectuals."

"Moroccan intellectuals dedicate themselves to tearing each other apart; the others are swallowed up in every day pursuits. You should hear them: 'Our salary increase is late!' 'Everything is so expensive!' 'The maid quit!' 'I've got to pick the kids up at school!' That's all they've got time for."

The phone was ringing when I walked in the house. Him again.

"Did you enjoy this evening?"

"Yes, thank you. Is that why you're calling?"

"Yes. Well, no. I've got a problem."

"What is it?"

"Let's talk about it later."

"Tell me now. Otherwise I'll worry about it."

"I'm wearied. That's all. Don't worry about it. It's an emotional thing. I can't sleep."

This was unsettling me. "We'll talk about it tomorrow, then," I said.

"OK, I'll see you before noon at your office."

"*Inshallah*!"

The next day was a beauty, as lovely as any I could remember. He came around eleven and even before he had sat down, he said, "It's the bureaucracy . . . . It's taking way too long to settle my affairs here."

"That's why you can't sleep?" I asked, disappointed.

"I can't stand this waiting. It's making me restless."

"Well, relax! Visit the town, read a book! You're on an unlimited, all expenses paid vacation! Get out and see the countryside. The road between Fes and Marrakech is fabulous this time of year. You wouldn't believe the fall colors."

At noon we left the office together. I drove him to his hotel and he invited me in to lunch, but I insisted on just a drink. We went in and sat on either end of a comfortable divan. A receptionist in uniform approached us immediately, leading two girls and grinning. The youngest had long loose yellow hair and was heavily made-up. She wore a tight T-shirt and the tightest jeans I had ever seen tucked into a pair of high-heeled black leather studded boots. They sat down uninvited to the evident consternation of my Saharan friend.

"We'll only stay until two," the older one announced, looking at her watch. He frowned disapproval. "One thirty then," she said as if bidding at auction. The younger one moved closer to him while the other began babbling her life story as if I deserved, or wanted, to know her business.

"A friend of my sister's married an American who's absolutely loaded. She was going to give us the address of this Jewish sorcerer in Meknes who helped her out, but she never did. Our oldest sister's married to a Japanese guy who worked at the embassy in Rabat. They're in Mauritius now. Maybe you have heard of it. It's an island somewhere. We go to the Hyatt all the time, thinking we'll meet a rich foreigner one of these days, but no such luck. We did meet a couple of Saudis once, who asked us to their rooms but the police are on the look-out, and we were afraid, it was too obvious. They asked for our phone number. Would you believe it? We don't even have a phone. I wish that bitch had given me her sorcerer's address. I'd share it with you. You're Aisha, aren't you? He talks about you all the time." She finished, nodding fondly toward my Saharan.

"I need to go," I said rising quickly.

"But you haven't touched your drink," he said, apologetic and embarrassed.

"We'll be leaving at one thirty. OK?" the older girl offered.

"You're leaving now," he said.

They left reluctantly, the younger tossing me hostile glances all the while. I stood looking into the hotel courtyard. He came next to me and said, "They're neighbors of a Saharan friend of mine who lives in the medina. I met them at his place. Their father's a soldier. They're poor people, actually."

"They're pathetic, at any rate," I said. "I've lived in Rabat all my life and had never encountered such girls till I met you. You're fresh off the plane and look who you've found. And you have the nerve to moralize against Moroccan women!? These two are dangerous, I'm warning you. They've got no religion, no direction, nothing to lose and they'll do absolutely anything. Didn't you see how the younger one was dressed?"

"She's a religious girl. She told me so."

"Those pants she's wearing tell you all you need to know about her religion. If the fundamentalists got hold of her, they'd stone her."

"In that case," he said triumphantly, "why were you defending those girls in bikinis, we saw on the beach?"

"I didn't say they were religious."

An expression of profound worry came over his face, and he put his hand to his head.

"I lost it. The money is gone." He groaned.

"What do you mean?"

"I lent a sister of theirs who married a Japanese guy a large sum of money. Her husband had sent her back to

Rabat on a one-way ticket. She begged me to help her get a return ticket to Mauritius and I took pity on her. She swore she'd pay me. Another difficult love story."

As if it was your money to give, I thought to myself. Oh well, public funds going back to the people, I guess. "You are insane!" I said. "Here you are with no job, and you lend money to people you don't even know."

"But I do know them. I visited their house. We ate couscous together."

"Big deal. It's not exactly a guarantee on your loan, is it? They couldn't return the money even if they wanted to. I told you these types were dangerous. Didn't you see the way that girl was dressed?"

"I've told you, she said she was religious."

"Islam forbids provocative exposure in public. Ever heard of Islam?"

"No," he snapped, angry and mocking.

"What do you believe in, anyway?" He stared at me wide-eyed and I lost my temper. "What are you? Christian? Jew? Buddhist?"

"I'm a heretic," he snarled. "How does that suit you?"

Before I could respond, he was summoned to the desk by a phone call from Tenerife. He went, massaging his temples with his fingers.

I paced a while, then looked back into the garden where it was pouring with rain, then paced some more. "I'll wait one more minute," I told myself, and went back to the window.

The rain had let up. I could hear drops falling on the leaves. An isolated heavy drop spattered on the glass. I watched a pair of amorous pigeons at play on the lip of a white marble fountain. I went back to the divan and sat down. He came back and practically fell into his seat, holding his forehead.

"I have a headache."

"I do too," I said rising and putting on my coat. "I'm leaving. Goodbye."

That night I dreamed about the two white doves in the courtyard. I was watering a rosebush and somehow the birds got splashed with mud. Feeling a deep sadness, I took my dress off to wipe them clean, but when I approached they parted and flew off in opposite directions. I turned my head from side to side feeling regret and grief, wishing I could bring them back together.

Two weeks went by before he showed up again at the office. He barged in and said, "How are you?"

"All right. How are *you*?"

He said he had some good news. He had been hired by the Ministry of Foreign Affairs, and posted to the Moroccan Embassy in Madrid.

"Congratulations," I said coolly. Then he said he wanted to invite me to a farewell meal.

"Will you come?"

"I'll come."

"Lunch or dinner?"

"Whichever is better for you."

"Which would be more appropriate, religion-wise?"

So we'd returned to the thorny issue of religion. I ignored the antagonism. "Religion-wise, lunch is better. Tomorrow?" I said.

"No, tomorrow is the feast."

"Really?! I was wondering what that bleating all over Rabat was."

"Let's do it now!"

We walked to a restaurant nearby. He leaned his head back in his chair, pressing his hair with both hands. His face appeared from a new angle. It was as if I had never seen it before. He crossed his hands behind his head. Our eyes met for a loaded, embarrassed moment. He looked away.

"I cannot believe you didn't know that it's the feast tomorrow."

"I'm out of it."

"Why?"

"Tired. Worn out."

"Oh? Why?"

I said it was because I didn't like my job and he pretended to believe me.

"Leave it, why don't you?"

I told him I had a debt I wanted to pay off first.

"You?" he said. "I thought you were well-off, one of those rich civil servants."

"You know nothing about me," I said harshly, "or

about anything else, for that matter. You're a sucker for appearances. A teenage girl can get the better of you. You're guillible. Do you know what guillible means?"

His lips tightened.

"No." He said bitterly. "We know nothing. We need you to teach us."

Thus ended the farewell lunch, a sour note on a magnificent clear October day in 1991, one year after the Gulf War debacle in Iraq.

A letter arrived in early November:

Aisha,

I am finally settled in here and you are the first person I have written to. Actually, settling in is not that big a deal for me. We are not exactly nomads anymore, but we do live like tortoises, with our homes on our backs.

Here I am in a new office and I am bored already. It is like being inside a moving van. My colleagues are all from the north, so-called Hispanophones. They resent my boredom and tell me I am so used to idleness and desert life that I cannot handle an office. They think they are quite sophisticated, but make plenty of inane remarks. "You were spoiled by the Spanish down there in the desert," they tell me. "Is it true they paid you just to sit around all day under a tent sipping tea?" That to roars of laughter and more insults. They are a vulgar lot, really. You would not believe the obsceneties they use, though I suppose you can find them easily enough in your modern literature.

I didn't really understand what you meant when you said you only did your job for the money. Now I know. "Office work is the slavery of the twentieth century," wrote al-Aqqad, God bless him! A keen intellect who refused to breathe anything less than the air of freedom.

The embassy has found me a furnished flat in a quiet neighborhood. I have written the address below. Write to me. Do not forget I need you.

Karim

Madrid, 7 November 1991

I slipped the letter into my bag, where it stayed for weeks. I was about to fulfil a lifelong dream and take a trip to Andalusia. Spain is next-door to us, but we rarely get there, while tourists from all over the world flock to it. As the saying goes, "Those who live near Mecca don't make the pilgrimage."

Rabat train station is a fine piece of architecture. I have to admit that the most artfully constructed public buildings in this town are those left by the French: the Bank of Morocco, the post office, the courthouse, the train station. Of course one must remember that the French were building these structures for themselves, since they had no intention of leaving. They even forbade Moroccans to use the main entrance to the station.

Once I participated in a seminar on resistance literature at an American university. We were supposed to be tracing the racist character of colonialism through various literary texts. At one point, I was led to observe, "Of course, this is no different from what Israel is doing to the Palestinians with your support, or from what you did to the Native Americans. You just come from Europe, take the land, and make second-class citizens out of the rightful occupants." People in the room looked stunned. I had not realized till then, that for them colonialism was an exclusive specialty of the Europeans.

As we were leaving the room a young woman remarked, "You're certainly outspoken!" Her voice held a disapproving edge. I asked someone else to explain to me what 'outspoken' means. "It is a way of describing someone with a big mouth," I was told.

The train moved, the benches, travelers and pillars on the platform withdrew. We emerged from a tunnel into a landscape strewn with black plastic bags, piles of garbage and discarded tools. A shanty town appeared, looking all the world like a refugee camp. I saw a woman sitting by the rails cradling a baby on her lap. Beside her a blanket was spread out to dry. Then a dump sending up strands of noxious smoke, a wasteland flapping with the ubiquitous plastic bags caught like ragged banners on every weed, where skinny sheep dusted black as charcoal-vendors grazed on dust.

"Shanty towns are a disease of the third world," an

expert in urban development from Glasgow once told me.

"Surely Europe has poor people. What do you call the places where they live?"

"We have poor people, but they don't live in tin shacks. That's inconceivable." He went on to express surprise at the scarcity of highways in Morocco.

"Isn't that justified?' I argued. "You say yourself that Morocco is a poor country."

"It's not justified, The raw materials are available and labour is cheap," was his diplomatic reply.

There's such a big difference between analysing a country's problems in a conference room and living with them in front of your nose. What I saw out of the window was lucky to be designated "third" world. They probably ought to invent new classes.

At Bensliman an old, slender countrywoman with an eagle nose boarded the train, followed by an emaciated young man. "Can you believe it?" she was yelling. "My son put me on the train to Fes! 'Get in!' He told me. And he's supposed to be switched on. That's what they call him. Switched on!" She apparently liked the expression, which she must have gleaned from the radio. A man from the Rif mountains, sitting nearby, asked the young man, "Did you get on the wrong train too?"

"Yes," he said unwillingly.

The pair found seats just behind the man from the Rif, who struck up further conversation with the woman.

"Going to see relatives in Tangier?"

"Yes, my son's children. He lives in Casablanca."

"Why don't you keep the children with you?"

"Heaven forbid! Anyway, his first wife is in Tangier. I married him off too young. It didn't work, so he got another wife from Fes. When she told him to move to Casablanca, he moved to Casablanca. 'Move here, move there!' If she told him to die he would die. I told him not to move there, and she said I should keep out of their way! So he bought a house in Casablanca. He paid more than twenty million for it."

The station at al-Qasr splits the face of the town like a countrywoman's tattoo. The train stopped and was overrun by a horde of young vendors. "Peanuts!" "Butter milk! Guaranteed fresh!" "Boiled eggs!" The old woman was having a heated argument with a boy over the price of something. A big man in a brown suede jacket came through clutching a brief case as if he were a normal traveler. In fact he was asking for money, booming out his pitch: "May God destroy those who have treated me unjustly!"

"Good grief," the old lady said, "beggars everywhere, on the bus, on the train. They'll be following us onto the planes next!"

The platform was packed with people and their large bundles wrapped in plastic.

"Smugglers!" declared the old lady.

"Produce, I bet," said the man. "As for hashish, they take it out by night from isolated beaches. I hear the government's talking about making it illegal to grow. If people can't grow it in the fields they'll do it in pots on their rooftops. That stuff grows anywhere."

"It's blessed!" remarked the old lady with a loud laugh. And we were off. I thought of smugglers and hashish till we came into Tangier. The train slowed and changed rhythm. The sea came up smack against the mountains. A line of hotels appeared on the road opposite, the tops of the palm trees waving in the wind of the strait and, at last, the city on the hills.

"Tangier the high!" exclaimed the old lady, repeating the words of a popular song. The train rattled and exhaled. Big mysterious bundles again crowded the platform. There was still plenty of daylight left, so I dropped my bags at a hotel and hired a big white Mercedes taxi.

"One hundred dirhams gets you the full tour," the driver told me. "The cave, the strait, Cap Spartel and the mountain. It's a hundred and fifty for tourists, a hundred for you. My name is Sa'id."

"Nice to meet you."

"We'll start with the cave of Hercules, the giant who dug the Strait of Gibraltar."

"According to legend," I felt it necessary to add.

"Hercules came from the United States."

"Oh? When was that?"

"It's ancient history."

"The United States didn't exist in ancient history. Did it?"

"I mean America, the continent."

"I thought he came from the East."

"Well, he came. That's the important thing. He left his footprint in a rock. I'll take you to see it if you like. It's as long as a man's arm. He was a giant, after all. You can get your picture taken down in the cave in front of the opening out on to the sea. You'll come out in silhouette, because of the light in the background. Tourists love it."

"They enjoy taking pictures of their shadows?"

"Tourists will do anything. They ride camels and look at the place where the Mediterranean meets the Atlantic."

"I don't see it!" I told Sa'id when we got there. "Where's the place where the sea meets the ocean?"

"It's there but it's clearer if you're looking down from an airplane. Is this your first time in Tangier?"

"Yes."

"What do you think of it?"

"I'm surprised to see so many expensive mansions, all these red-tiled villas overlooking the sea. People are always saying the north is poor, that that's why France let Spain have it. Where do people get this kind of money, in that case? There are no tin shacks, none of the squalor you see in other cities."

"They exist, all right. You just don't see them. We sweep them under the rug for the tourists." He used classical Arabic impressively, suggesting that northerners deserved their reputation for being a poor but cultured people. I told him as much.

"We're descendents of the Andalusians, after all," he remarked proudly.

He drove cautiously up the mountainous road, shifting down for the steep inclines.

"This mountain was something else in its heyday. It was our Beverly Hills. Most of these villas were built by Europeans, the British mainly. Nowadays they're built by rich Moroccans or people from the Gulf. Once a committee of Gulf Arabs met with our city council representatives, and asked what they could do for Tangier. 'Build a mosque and a school,' the council said. Too bad they didn't say university. We'd have got one!"

The road was empty, the villas were silent in their green cloak of pines against the blue of sky and sea.

"I wouldn't call it Beverly Hills," I told Sa'id. "It's more like Greece, or Nice even; the sea, the mountains, the pines, the red-tiled roofs." I spotted a minaret inside the walls of a large villa. "Private mosques even!" I said incredulously.

"Oh yes," said Sa'id. "But rest assured, they've got a bar next door to their mosque."

I quoted the Qur'an: "*Thou shalt never stand therein. Surely a mosque built from the first day out of piety is worthier that thou shouldst stand therein*. What's that?" I asked, pointing to a burnt out villa.

"That one belongs to a hashish dealer. Someone torched it. Pay-back time."

"Who would do a thing like that?"

"Gangs. Who do you think?"

"There are gangs?"

"Where're you from, woman?"

"I was born in Meknes, but I went to school in Rabat and that's where I've lived ever since."

"I mean what country are you from? This is Morocco. Where have you been?"

"I've been here, but I've never heard anything about organized crime. Radio and TV don't talk about it."

"I can assure you there are gangs. Once I attended a wedding outside Tetouan, up in the mountains, and they came in and kidnapped the bride in broad daylight, right off the street. I wouldn't have believed it if I hadn't seen it happen with my own eyes. It was like those pictures you get on carpets, showing a veiled horseman swooping down to snatch a woman and gallop away. She was taken from right in front of my eyes. Her father was a hashish dealer too. More pay-back."

"It sounds as if any big money around here is dirty money."

"That's why they need to wash it clean. One way is to build villas."

And I had just got done comparing Tangier to Nice! Monaco, built on gambling money, would have been more appropriate. I was puzzled by what makes dirty money so abundant.

*

Crossing the strait was hardly a voyage of Sindbad, just a few uneventful hours. The ferry was crowded with Moroccans heading back to their less-than-elegant lives in Europe. Many were sick over the side.

The moment we landed, everything was different: cars, people, buildings, parks, cafes, shops. The world went from third to first. Their world! Knowledgeable, powerful, developed, secular, the world of the pharaoh.

I recalled the observations made by my insolent Saharan: "Here in Morocco, people on the street look shabby. You wouldn't see people going around like that in Spain. The amount and level of poverty here is appalling."

"Rabat was not always this way," I had answered. "One used to feel embarrassed to walk down the avenue in casual dress, because everybody looked so distinguished. But then, Rabat isn't Morocco, and things aren't what they were."

To enter Granada is a unique experience, all the more so if you are an Arab. It brings a bitter lump to the throat. It is like going back to a home you were forced to leave after a divorce. The Alhambra is pure Umayyad poetry, untranslatable. The pillars are so elegantly slender. The phrase "None is conqueror save God," in graceful Kufic script, is carved in stone, carved in my heart.

I took in every doorway, every window, the walls, ceilings, pillars, corridors, fountains, courtyards. My eye followed every line, every hollow, soaking it up until the tears came.

There was a flamenco dancer in the hotel that evening, who looked just like a Rabati girl I had once been at school with. She had the same fair complexion, the slight plumpness, the dark eyes, the dark, braided hair, the same tall, graceful body, the austere smile, the same flower behind her ear. We used to tease her: "Hey! Do you still have the keys to your place in Granada hanging on the wall of your house? When are you planning to go back?"

"No, no," she would say. "We threw the keys away a long time ago."

My Saharan visitor had said that there were still people in Andalusia who professed Islam, secretly of course. He said they had mosques under their houses in Granada, Cordoba and Seville. He told a story about a Spaniard who had converted to Islam during a visit to Rabat. He had been walking down the avenue in the medina, toward the minaret, when he heard the call to prayer. He said it felt as if the call was coming from inside him, as if he was simply acknowledging a voice from the past.

Thinking about the Saharan, I realized that we were under the same sky. I pulled his letter out of my purse and reread it.

That night in my hotel I couldn't sleep. I sat up late wondering how we Arabs had managed to hang onto all the lands we had conquered except for those of al-Andalus. Why Andalusia? These thoughts led me to compare, strangely, the Arabs in Andalusia with Israel. Like Israel, al-Andalus was surrounded, implanted in soil that was not its own. Certainly, it lasted for eight centuries, but where is all that now? Eight hundred years of worry and vigilance, and at the first opportunity al-Andalus became the palaces of Spain, a tune in a *muwashah* song, a nuance in a verse of poetry, an essay in a book, a wound in the Arab spirit. It couldn't have lasted even if it had gone on for another eight hundred years; its presence in the midst of the enemy, its dreams of staying and of the safety of its borders, all as surreal as a UNESCO play.

I stood in front of the window and looked out onto a gloomy rooftop in the middle of which was a construction like the country shrines of Morocco with a few plants and flowers around it in metal containers brushed with lime. I imagined for a moment that I was on a rooftop in the old city of Rabat. Then I remembered:

> I am in Seville. From the narrow window in my room I can see the city's whitewashed roofs, the laundry stretched out to dry. For a minute I thought I was in Fes. The walls and gates make you think you are in Rabat. The tilework is pure Moroccan. If you were here, you would cry to see the lovely world your ancestors had to leave behind.

This trip had been an occasion to reflect on the way we Arabs have handled our occupation of other lands. We referred to the colonized territory as *misr* (city) and to colonization as *fath* (opening).

True, such colonization did not bring the scale of refugee camps, deportations, imprisonments, and home demolition, that define Israel today. True, the Arabs were relatively tolerant and relatively involved in their actions. They did not make the inevitable mistakes of those colonizers who acted as absentee landlords. But there is no getting around the facts. Colonization, no matter how "gentle," amounts to the taking of someone else's land, and the imposing by force of an alien language and culture.

I woke up the next morning still burdened by my thoughts. "This is absurd," I said. "Here I am, killing myself, crying over the spilt milk of Andalusia when I'd be better off in Madrid or Barcelona." So I went to a travel agent who strongly recommended Madrid, mainly because my time was limited, and Barcelona, she said, was too far. I followed her advice, but wish I had not, for reasons that have nothing to do with either city.

Madrid is elegant, a city of tasteful buildings with balconies in bloom, and magnificent plazas with statues and fountains. I was reminded of both Paris and Rome. As I gazed at the profusion of trees my thoughts turned back to an interview I had seen on Moroccan TV. A government official had been asked why so little attention was given to the aesthetics of planting trees. "Well," he'd replied. "If aesthetics are not taken into consideration when building new houses or planning a new urban community, why should we be expected to worry about trees? Aesthetics are fine in the developed world, but we aren't at that stage here yet." With more than a thousand years of refinement and civilization at his back, he was still able to say, "Not yet. We aren't there yet."

"Moron!" I had shouted at the TV, as if they could hear. "What's your plan when we do get there? To go back and demolish the ugliness you've accomplished?"

A foreign friend once said to me, "I look at the traditional arts in Morocco, and am amazed at the beauty and quality of the work. Then I look at the pictures on the walls of the average Moroccan home today and am appalled at the utter lack of taste."

I bought a ticket for one of the guided tours, but having a few hours to myself, I did the inevitable. I got a cab, gave Karim's letter to the driver and showed him the address. I stared at the letter until we stopped and the driver pointed to an apartment building. I paid and got out.

The area was exactly as I had imagined it; spacious streets and tall trees. I stepped inside the building and was hit by a wave of anxiety. At the apartment door, I took a deep breath and rang the bell. A young girl opened almost at once. She was small and slim, with fair, loose hair down her back. "She'd look like me," I thought, "if not for her complexion."

"Sorry," I said in French. "I must have the wrong place."

"Who were you looking for?" she asked kindly, in a thick accent.

"His name is Karim. He's with the Moroccan Embassy."

"You've got the right place, then. And who are you?"

"My name's Aisha. I'm from Morocco. I'll be in Madrid a few days, and just thought I'd surprise him."

"Come in." she said. She opened the door wide and followed me inside. "I'm Karim's wife. I couldn't be with him in Morocco because I was nine months pregnant, or I'd probably have met you. Can I get you something to drink?" she called from the kitchen.

I could not speak for fear my voice would crack. I went out on the balcony, as if I had not heard her question, as if all I wanted was to have a look around the neighborhood. She entered the room with two drinks and called me back inside. I slid the glass door of the balcony closed, and thanked her for the drink.

"I've never been to Morocco myself," she said. "But my nephew was in Tangier last summer. He went to the beach and somebody stole his clothes. The poor kid had to go back to his hotel in his swimming trunks."

"How old is your nephew?"

"Seventeen."

"That's young! He shouldn't have been there on his own."

"He says they don't have parking meters over there. Instead you pay a man standing on the street when you want to park your car."

"That's true. It makes for more jobs. There's a lot of unemployment, you know. So when did you and Karim get married?"

"A little over a year ago. I had Amin while Karim was in Morocco."

She stood up, left the room and returned with a baby in diapers, talking to it in Spanish. She extended the tiny bundle toward me with a trusting, familiar gesture, just as any Moroccan mother would have done. "*Bismillah!*" I said, holding the child with extreme care, as if he were made of eggs. "He's beautiful!" I said sincerely. "He'll be a blend of East and West, *inshallah*. He's a little over a month old, I'd guess."

"Yes. Can you believe it, he's already been on a plane journey! I'm eighteen and I'd never been on a plane before in my life. I'd never even left Tenerife till last month in fact."

"What's your name?"

"Maria."

"Were you working with a human rights group in the Canaries, by any chance?"

"No, what makes you say that? I've never really had a job. I was in school when I married Karim. We met under unusual circumstances, to say the least. He ran into me with his car. I wasn't badly injured, but he kept visiting me in the hospital. We were engaged before they let me out."

A key sounded in the door.

"That will be Karim," she said. "Won't he be surprised?"

"Won't he just?" I said through clenched teeth. I handed

the baby back to her and she returned it to its crib. The man stood in the doorway, looking at me and rubbing his eyes. Maria came back and I got up to take my leave.

"But you two haven't said a word!" she protested in her friendly, innocent way. "Did the surprise work?"

"More than expected," I said.

In the elevator, I tore the letter into pieces. They felt heavy in my hand, until I threw them away in a litter barrel.

Back at the hotel, I was the first to get on the tour bus. A Senegalese man sat down next to me. We stopped in the main plazas and parks, at the university, and at the museum. All I remember from the Prado is a painting, probably by Goya, and a tiny, frail, gray-haired man who was doing the commentary. The painting was of a group of children standing at the base of a haystack, looking up.

"These children would like to climb," the man said, "but they cannot. The haystack is slippery."

I do not remember much else about the tour. The guide said something about there being over a hundred varieties of rose in one of the parks. I sat with the Senegalese man at a small snack bar, among beds and trellises filled with their hundred varieties or rose.

"Are you married?" he asked me.

"No."

"Why not?"

"Good question."

"What's the good answer?"

"It's a long story, I'm afraid."

"You probably just haven't found the right match yet."

"On the contrary. I have found the right match on several occasions. Once it was with a government official who turned out to be married. Just the other day he was on TV news, inaugurating some new mosque outside the capital. Another time, it was with another high-ranking official in government. And believe it or not, he was on the same newscast, distributing wheelchairs to handicapped children. He too seemed an excellent match at one time."

"What went wrong?"

"Ask a fortune-teller, ask fate. I don't have a clue."

"How did you meet him?"

"At a conference. There was nothing remarkable about him. In fact, I found him rather ugly. I sensed in him the full set of 'attributes': arrogance, stubbornness, harshness, superiority and scorn toward women. All the defects, you know, of the typical third-world official. He had hard, tight features, as if his face was made of some substance that could not be stretched into a smile. I used to look at him and imagine a heart-shaped rock under his ribs. I have never seen anyone look so hard. I had thought such faces were reserved for history books, people like the pharoah, Hitler or al-Hajjaj. You wouldn't know al-Hajjaj, I guess. He was a tyrant from the first Islamic dynasty.

"Anyway, after that conference, he asked me to come by his office where I was allegedly needed to translate some

126

document or other. I went and by the time I had left the office, every one of those defects I had credited him with, was transformed into its opposite. Ugliness turned to beauty in the blink of an eye."

"Magic! And then?"

"And then, nothing. I tried and tried to get through to him. He kept holding back. The struggle lasted a year, until I finally gave up. I still don't understand what happened. We were very compatible. And I know for a fact he was very interested in me. Why did he behave like that? Maybe you can tell me?"

"I don't think he'd have strung you along like that if he had been really serious."

The waiter came by and I asked for a Schweppes Tonic in a can.

"I drink tonic when I'm heartsick," I explained to my companion, and started watching a couple of boys in navy-blue shorts playing nearby. They wore school uniforms and their socks came up to the knee. I thought: You cannot climb the haystack, boys. It's slippery! Then, I wondered why I had so confided in this stranger, and why, if I was in such a confiding state of mind, I had elected to skip over the utter fiasco that had reached its climax a few hours before.

6

I knew Aisha at school, though I am sure if she were to meet me now, I would mean nothing to her. Yet I do remember her, in spite of my failing memory. Her beauty revealed itself in every aspect. You felt it in her conduct, movement, the way she spoke, the tone of her voice, her laughter. It slipped into your heart and took root there. She lit up any gathering and drew eyes as a magnet draws iron filings.

Aisha was intelligent too, and that gave rise to mixed feelings in her peers. Their admiration was often tainted by jealousy, though Aisha generally seemed oblivious. I remember how one of the girls ran up breathlessly saying, "Aisha skipped a whole year! She took the exam a year early and passed! Can you believe it?"

"God preserve us!" I thought, seeing the contempt on the girl's face. "We'll kill our geniuses with the jealousy in our eyes if we cannot get them with the sword."

"Say '*tabaraka Allah*'!" I told her, to protect Aisha from her evil eye.

"Why wish God's blessing on her?" she stammered in reply. "It's us you ought to be worried about. Here we are, studying day in, day out, and Aisha skips a year in one day. Why? Why her and not us? What's she got that we don't?"

Intelligence, I thought immediately. If her brains were weighed against the brains of all of you lot put together, hers would easily tip the balance. What I actually said was, "For God's sake! If we can't succeed ourselves, we can at least let someone else do it."

Even they could not miss my point.

"Jealousy is a human disease," said one of them. "It's not exclusively Moroccan. Strauss was jealous of his own son you know. So, don't go making the rest of the world out to be angels."

I walked away, asking God to protect Aisha, confident that He would listen to the prayers of a well-wisher.

That was the year I got married to a *faqih* and traded in my modern wardrobe for a *djellaba*. I renounced most of the things that had adorned my life till then. No more high heels, handbags, stockings or make-up; just a pair of simple flowing shirts to wear and launder in turn, and a headscarf to be removed only when I went to the public bath. I turned my back on society and entered the world of the cooking pot, brazier, and washbasin. Before long I was finding it difficult even to read a newspaper or walk in the street. I had married a *faqih*! As my poor, naive mother put it, "Religion preserves a man and holds him in check, for nothing destroys a woman like betrayal."

I said "Amen!" to that, and accepted the role of being his wife. I too was naïve. We believed that a *faqih* was someone with a special knowledge of God's Book and the sayings of His Messenger, but we discovered otherwise. And I had interpreted the man's mother's impatience to match her son with me as eagerness to fulfill God's will. It was really nothing more than a maneuver to separate him from the *sherifa*, the woman he really desired. Once the deed was done, I heeded my mother's advice and accepted my fate.

"It's your lot," she said. "It's what was in store for you and you must stay with it, if only for the sake of your children. The olive tree is battered for its fruit." Then, she would heave a sigh, almost a moan and add, "It could have been worse."

I could not imagine how anything could possibly have

been worse. Perhaps that is what enabled me to weather the calamities to come. Then one night, Aisha appeared on television and I recognized her. She looked soberly elegant, as beautiful as ever, yet sad somehow. The subject of her talk was beyond me, yet I was drawn to it as one is drawn to a beautiful fabric without necessarily understanding how it is made. She referred to names that stirred in my memory like faces we know but cannot place, like traces of dreams we cannot remember: al-Mutanabbi, al-Naysaburi, al-Jahiz, al-Mas'udi, al-Ma'arri, al-Hamadani, al-Asma'i, al-Tabrizi. I shut my eyes and concentrated, until I could visualize the names, but they remained mere letters devoid of significance. As for her name, it sprang clear the instant the camera moved in on her face, which glowed like a full moon in the desert night.

"Aisha!" I cried. "Aisha who skipped a year of school!" The words flew from my mouth like boiling coffee, but my husband paid no attention or pretended not to, and I slipped to the rug where I sat cross legged before the television set, as I had that evening soon after the 1967 war, when Umm Kulthum was in Morocco to raise funds for the army, and her performance was broadcast live from Mohammed V theater.

"It's as if she were singing!" Once more my words shot out. "Now that's what I call an educated mind!" Aisha's presence enthralled me and I prayed that God protect her from the evil eye. "God bless her! She looks like a queen!" I did not care whether my husband's silence was true indifference or pretense to it.

"A woman's kingdom is her home," he muttered. "I'll bet you anything she's dying to exchange that nonsense for a husband. A woman should learn just enough to raise her children and say her prayers. And that's more than enough!"

Right! I thought bitterly. Like this happy kingdom you've given me!

Where do they get these notions? A woman should learn just enough to raise her children and say her prayers? Yet the Messenger of God himself, God's prayer and peace be upon him, said, "Seeking knowledge is the religious duty of every Muslim man and woman." A religious duty, no less, like fasting and prayer, not merely a privilege or right. But men like my husband make use of whatever they can to shore up their crumbling hold on the world.

He had deflated me. The joy I had felt on seeing Aisha dissipated and fear came in its place, a heavy, dark, painful throb. Ever since I married such mood swings have been common. And there is the forgetfulness. God help me! In the time it takes me to get across the room to the front door, I forget what it was I intended to do. When my mother-in-law asks me to do something, I go around whispering the words so I won't forget.

One day in the public bath, I was unable to find my towel. I had put it in a plastic bag and had put the bag in one of the buckets in the first of the three chambers. When I went in to get it, it was not there, and I could not help but suspect, God forgive me, the two girls sitting close by. The woman in charge was sympathetic and fed my suspicions. "They'd steal it, wouldn't they?" She said. "You should've left it with me."

Normally, I would have let the matter drop, but I knew my mother-in-law would nag me about it until I'd get a headache. So I went back to my spot in the middle chamber, my anxiety mounting and looked down, and there it was, the towel in the bucket. I had taken it there myself from the first chamber and had not even remembered doing so.

And the sleeplessness. My eyes stay open until the muezzin's first invocation before the dawn prayer, and then I'll spend the day distracted and dazed, doing my best to conceal it from my mother-in-law whose taunts and laughter follow me around like a whip. Easy for her to laugh! May she never laugh again! May she be cursed with insomnia. I pull my resentment together and direct it toward her, but I can't touch her. My evil eye never works. It is like trying to write with water.

"It's strange. It's not normal," my mother said about my sleeplessness and forgetfulness.

"I'd like to know what witchcraft she's using." I said.

"Don't talk like that!" said my mother. "God will undo her spells. Satan, may God curse and disgrace him, has taken her from light to darkness."

My mother took me to a doctor who kept prescribing sleeping pills, until she asked him angrily, "Isn't there anything else you can do?"

His answer was that there is no way to X-ray or operate on the inner self.

"At least the *faqih* prescribes incense or amulets, or reads a verse of the Qur'an."

"Then go to the *faqih!*" He spoke in earnest and added, as if to confirm that he was not making fun of us, "Medical science cannot cure everything. A doctor's knowledge is limited. There's nothing wrong with trying a traditional cure if you think it will help."

"I'm surprised you would tell us that, a doctor like you," said my mother. The doctor explained that he had seen traditional medicine work on supposedly hopeless cases. He said that if the will of God could cause disease, it could certainly cause it to disappear as well. Including *that which was brought down on the two angels in Babel, Harut, and Marut,*" he said, quoting the Qur'an.

"Witchcraft, you mean?"

He nodded and overrode my objections by quoting various verses from the Qur'an that mention witchcraft.

"If a thing is written in the Qur'an," he noted, "we believe that it is true, like the parting of the Red Sea by Moses. Who otherwise could accept that Jesus brought the dead to life? The Qur'an tells us it was so, and we believe."

He selected a large volume from the shelf behind him, cleaned his glasses and began leafing through the pages. "The chapter on magic. The evidence is here in the Hadith, as witnessed by 'Ubaid ibn Isma'il, Abu Usama, Hisham, his father, and Aisha, the Prophet's wife. *The Prophet had such a strong spell cast on him that he imagined he had done something he hadn't done . . .*"

"Like me!" I put in, reminded of the towel and bucket in the bath house, "except that I do things I can't remember having done!"

"Sufyan says this is stronger than magic." The doctor read on, ignoring me: *"One day, the Prophet was in my room. He prayed for a long time, then said to me, 'God has heard my prayers.'*

"*'What is it, O Messenger of God?' I asked.*

"*'Two men came to me,' he answered, 'One sat at my head, the other at my feet, and one said to the other, "What's causing this man's pain?" "A spell is cast on him," the other answered.'"*

The doctor peered at us over his glasses. "Those two men," he explained, "were Gabriel and Michael and the spell was the work of a sorcerer. It was cast by Labid ibn al-'Asam, a Jew from the Banu Zuraiq."

"That's probably why people think Jews make the best sorcerers," my mother observed. He ignored her interruption as he had mine and read on. *"The spell was cast with a comb, a lock of hair, and pollen from the male date-palm.* Well, we know the comb," the doctor explained. "And as for the hair, it refers to those strands that come out in the comb when it is passed through the hair. And the pollen of the male date-palm: that's the pollen the bees collect for making their honey."

"May God keep you!" my mother said. "It's rare for a doctor these days to combine scientific and religious knowledge."

"The government's policy is to restrict religion to mosques or religious institutions. In fact, it should be taught in schools and universities for the benefit of young people. Religion must be allowed to interact with secular science if we are ever to be free from the illusion of materialism. If I were running things, I'd insist on it. Can you believe it? We're still using the French curriculum from 1912 in some places!"

"Where did we get to?" said my mother, pointing to the volume.

"To the bit about the date-palm pollen," said the doctor. "'*So he said, "It is in Zurwan's well, which is in the Prophet's city of Medina, in the orchard of the Banu Zuraiq."' The Prophet went there with his companions and looked at the well surrounded by palms. He came back and said 'By God, it's as if the water of the well had been mixed with henna and the crowns of the palm trees were the heads of devils.' Then I said to the Prophet, 'Did you exorcise it?' 'No,' he said. 'God has cured me, and I feared I would bring evil to the people.' Then the Prophet ordered the well to be filled in.*" And here the doctor finished reading from the book.

My house is a part of hell, a devil's workshop run by an old witch who puts spells on her son, who in turn makes his living by putting spells on other people.

"I only do it so he'll obey me," she tells her divorced daughter. "So he'll give me money and provide for the two of us. Even the judge's wife puts spells on her sons, after all. They're grown men but they bleat in her presence like frightened sheep. I only do it so he'll provide for us."

That's how she tries to justify her evil. The two of them talk in front of me as if I were not there, or did not speak Arabic. Right in front of me my mother-in-law will sprinkle some potion from an old jam jar onto part of the plate of food we're all about to eat from. She indicates the contaminated portion and says, "Take this downstairs and make sure this part is in front of Sidi Muhammad." And I glide down the stairs absent-mindedly, like someone under the effect of a narcotic or hypnosis. No force on earth could stop me from obeying her orders. Dear God!

Since we stopped going to the doctor, my mother has been reminding me each time we meet to read the Yassin chapter of the Qur'an before sleep and immediately on waking, and to breakfast with seven dates each morning. But I forget. Mother hardly comes to visit anymore, and when she does she refuses to touch food or drink, under the pretext that she is fasting.

When I told my mother the story about the dish of food, she didn't understand.

"What're you talking about?" she said.

"Those things are happening under my roof," I said.

138

"I thought it was another dream of yours. I've heard of women who oppress their daughters-in-law. Worse cases than yours and God destroys their minds. There was this woman who would meddle in her son's marriages and make him get a divorce every time. Well, one morning they found her in the kitchen tearing at the ceiling, the beams and sheets of tin and everything, until she had actually pulled the roof apart. And when they asked her what she was doing, she said, 'Looking for my purse.' Mark my words. The day will come when your mother-in-law will pay for what she's done. How much do you want to bet?"

Making bets was a favorite game of my mother's. As long as I can remember, she has said, "We're going to do, or not going to do, this or that, because I know what's going to happen. How much do you want to bet?"

I went ahead and bet, and my mother asked how I was feeling. I told her how sick at heart I feel, and about the headaches that are like a needle being pushed into my skull, and how the pain throbs like an electric current and goes on till the next needle hits. I described the stiffness in my neck and joints, the fatigue that hobbles me so that I go tottering around like an old woman, the dullness in my brain as if I have been thumped with a club, the sadness, the forgetfulness. I told her how the old woman insults me: "Look at her, standing there like a clod of dirt. She's in another world! Always chewing cud like a camel!" That last was in reference to a gum the doctor had prescribed for me.

"My reaction to her is always the same," I told my mother. "If this is the fate written for me, I accept it, but if it's the work of some sorcerer, may God avenge me! God fulfills the curse of the tyrannized. And there are two of us tyrannized in this case, the *sherifa* and me."

"Did you really say that to her?" my mother asked, incredulous.

"Well, no. Not exactly. But I said it in my heart."

At that my mother let out a whoop of laughter. It made me glad to think I had tickled her so. She wiped her eyes and took time to catch her breath.

"Goodness, how you make me laugh sometimes. So you gave her the finger from under your *djellaba*, did you? Just like Juha!" And she told a story I already knew, of Juha and the thief: "One night, Juha's wife woke him up to report that a thief had broken into the house. Juha took her hand and led her up on to the roof, saying, 'Just wait and see what I'll do to that wretch!' They crouched down on the roof, and whenever Juha's wife urged him to do something, he said, 'Just you wait! You'll see!' Meanwhile the thief cleaned out the house and disappeared. Eventually, Juha got up, and cautiously went downstairs again.

"'Well?' asked his wife, when he returned. 'What did you do?' 'I flipped him off from under my *djellaba*,' Juha replied."

As for the old woman, she was far from impotent. She did do something awful to the *sherifa*, her son's lover whose place I took. I heard the old witch gloating to her daughter over how the *sherifa* and her mother had gone to every fortune teller and *faqih* in town, to no avail.

"I'm sure they couldn't compete with you," I thought, sarcastically.

On the night of my wedding, the groom's family literally sneaked me through the back streets to the house, as if kidnapping me.

"It's not our custom to bring the bride home with a lot of fanfare," the old woman told me. The truth was that she was afraid of what the *sherifa* might do to stop the marriage, and did not want her to find out. Being an expert in the damage witchcraft could do, she did not want to be on the receiving end.

"If she were in Saudi Arabia they'd put her to death," my mother declared. "Your husband too, I'm afraid. That's the penalty for sorcery in Islam. A sword to the neck." And then poor soul, she said, "I wish those two were in Saudi Arabia, by God!"

"It would be better to wish there were true Islam in Morocco!" I retorted.

My mother put her finger to her lips, looked around her, and then whispered, "Walls have ears! Don't you know people go to jail for that kind of talk?"

This was back when independence was very new. We still had not heard about democracy or human rights or free speech or any of the other catchwords everyone uses these days. "Walls have ears" was a far more useful phrase to go by.

Well, the *sherifa* ended up emigrating to France carrying her disgrace in her belly. Her mother stayed behind in a dilapidated boarding house, cursing the old woman to the heavens. The *sherifa* is always on my mind. What could she possibly be doing now in France? France of all places!

One day I met a worn-out old woman at the shrine I go to. She was living in France and just over on a visit.

"We get pushed around plenty there," she told me. "Don't be fooled by appearances. Just because we come back shining and smiling and with a carload of stuff. We bathe for a week before coming back here. Eight days of scrubbing with Moroccan soap and bath mitts."

"Don't tell me," I said, "that you can find Moroccan soap and scrubbing mitts over there?"

"We've got everything there. '*Adouls*, *neggafas*, fortune-tellers, musicians. The works! Oh, yes. I knew this bloody French woman who had been divorced by her husband, a Moroccan, I won't say his name. He's big in government." She raised her hand as high as it would go to show just how big. "He divorced her ten years ago and still isn't remarried. You know why? That good-for-nothing piece of shit cast a spell on him to block his remarriage, that's why."

"What? How could she have known how to do that?"

"She was taught by Muslim women, so called. 'Muslim women' of this fourteenth Islamic century of ours. When the Messenger of God read about it, he closed the book he was reading and wept. And we still don't understand why the Jews defeated us."

"Yes, as if they were the true believers. But *Hajja*, how

could the Messenger of God have read those things in a book? He was illiterate. Your story can't be true I'm afraid. You realize that those who make false allegations about the Messenger of God risk hellfire?"

"Well, the responsibility rests on those who told the story."

I often wonder if the *sherifa*, had she married my husband would really have been any better off. Which one of us suffers the deepest disgrace, she under the tyranny of France or me under the tyranny of the old witch? At least in France there is no witchcraft to worry about. But how quickly I forget! The woman at the shrine said they had everything. As the proverb says, "When calamity reaches its peak one can only laugh." So we are exporting witchcraft now. Our own *fleurs du mal*, like the book by that French poet whose name I cannot remember any more.

Another woman at the shrine, who works as a cleaning lady in one of the ministries, had this story to tell: "There was this Moroccan woman, born in France, who came here without a word of Arabic. She was given a good position at the ministry where I work and didn't waste any time in starting an affair with the boss. Next thing you knew, they were married. He bought her a villa in Souissi but she wasn't satisfied. She wanted him to divorce his first wife. He told her he couldn't do that because she was his cousin, and took good care of his mother, and was the mother of his four children, and so on and so forth, but she kept pushing him. Well, he got upset and divorced her. So what did she do? I'll tell you what she did.

143

She put a spell on him. And all of a sudden he's nuts about her. He went back to her on his knees, and promised to divorce not only the cousin, but his own mother too if that was how she wanted it. It's true! And she couldn't speak a word of Arabic when she came to Morocco. Born and raised in France!"

"I told you!" piped up the old woman. "France has everything, fortune-tellers and all."

"No wonder the French don't like us," said the cleaning lady.

"But why doesn't God paralyze the hands of these sorcerers?" I asked. "May God forgive me!"

"God delays but does not forget," one remarked.

There was a time when I would say, "My life will begin when the old witch is dead. My life depends on her death." Now, here I am, dead as can be, while she still thrashes her way around the house. I cannot forgive her. I took my mother's bet out of compliance, the one that my marriage would be a sound and happy one. I can see the old woman coming to propose the match with her son, calling me "Lalla Umm Hani," saying how I would be her second daughter from that day on.

Around that time I had a dream. Whenever I have a dream it turns out to be true. When the old woman heard me make that claim, her face twisted with contempt and she said, "Pharaoh's dream turned out to be true too, you know, and he was certainly no saint."

In my dream, I saw a withered thorn tree inside the

house I grew up in, rooted near the front door. I tried to slip outside, but the tree reached for me. I looked for a support to lean on, but there was none. The leafless, branches, bristling with thorns stretched out like claws. Two of the thorns pierced my shirt. I pulled back, and peacefully removed the thorns.

When I told my mother about the dream I begged her not to tell me the thorns meant "husband." Whenever she interpreted my dreams, everything always came back to husbands.

"I dreamed about shoes," I would say.

"Shoes signify a husband," she would say. Shoes, cars, belts, sprigs of mint; they were all symbols for the husband according to my mother.

So, she gave my dream a lot of thought, but said finally, "Husband. The thorn is an obstruction, from which the mercy of God has saved you."

A little later, just as she was asking whether I wanted to bet that it would be a successful marriage, we both heard a snatch of an 'Abd al-Halim song coming from somewhere, bringing these words of distress: "He who tries to undo her plaits will be lost! Lost! Lost!" We stood there stunned, and I saw the thorn tree reaching for me, like a piece of film running over and over in my mind.

When the doctor gave up on me I started visiting the shrine regularly. Whenever I feel depressed, I put on my *djellaba* and go there. I sit alone in the dark, incense perfumed interior, or join the *dhikr* ceremony until the shackles on me burst apart and my grief is drawn back like a curtain. Then I go home with a light step, the way I used to feel so many years ago.

Yesterday there were just two other women at the shrine. One was lying down, the other sat cross-legged, gnawing the end of a French loaf. I sat near them and the drift of their talk caught my ear. The one who was eating said, "On Fridays they bring couscous to every shrine but this one. I wonder why that is."

"They used to," the other one said. "But the man in charge kept taking it home."

"That food is meant for the poor and hungry."

"Shame on him."

"He forgets that tomorrow he may die, if not today. May he die under torture!"

"They don't even let you sleep here at night!"

"They do at Sidi Ben 'Asher."

"Yes, they do, but it's in a room and you have to pay. They still won't let you sleep in the shrine."

"And you need I.D."

"There's a guy there who sometimes sells fish. You give him a hundred rials and he'll give you a lapful."

"Fried or fresh?"

"Fried. How much were those bananas you bought the other day? A hundred rials?"

"You must be joking! They were 260, by God."

"You used to be able to get them for a hundred."

"That was last year."

"I used to get a kilo of bananas and a kilo and a-half of apples. At least oranges are still cheap."

"They're a hundred rials, too. You call that cheap?"

"What I wouldn't give for a fresh glass of orange juice!"

Such talk took me away from my problems. It was still going through my head as I walked home. To think that some people must concentrate their whole beings on getting enough to eat! "Death is the same for all," says a poet, "but the causes are different."

And then there is my mother's phrase again: "The olive tree is battered for its fruit. Endure it, for the sake of your children." And haven't I endured? For nearly twenty years, since Yasir was born. We named him after 'Arafat, an apt choice I guess, since I have become like the Palestinians, living on hope alone. I wake up and say, "Tomorrow," and when tomorrow comes, I say, "Tomorrow," again.

Once the doctor asked me, "What makes you happy?"

I searched hard for a reply but could not come up with one.

"What do you like in life," he tried again.

This time an answer came quickly.

"Nothing."

"Housework? Do you enjoy that! Shopping? Music? . . ." he continued his list and I shook my head each time.

"Do you often cry like this?"

I nodded and struggled to control myself.

147

"I feel like a collapsed building. I feel I don't belong to this life. It's as if I'm in exile. Reality for me is in dreams and hallucinations, whether I'm asleep or awake."

"Isn't there anything at all that interests you? An idea, perhaps? Some issue you feel close to?"

"The Palestinian people," I said. "I feel their pain and it hurts me. I want it to stop. I want the killing of those children to stop, even if there is nothing in it for me. Do you see? I mean to say that, given the choice of ending my own agony or theirs, I'd choose to end theirs."

"Good then!" exclaimed the doctor. "You aren't entirely cut off from the world. There's hope in that!"

I told him that I had had another dream, and he pulled out his recorder and switched it on, eagerly, as if I were Shehrazade, getting ready to entertain for the night. But his technology and science were of little help to me, and when at last he acknowledged defeat, I realized I had no refuge save God. Just last night, I had another dream. It went like a screenplay to an American film.

The dream. Scene one: An interior. A shot of my back. Daylight. I am walking down a long corridor. I might be in a hospital. The end of the hall appears far ahead. A voice is calling me: "Umm Hani! Hey! Umm Hani!"

I look to my right and left, up and down, startled, perplexed, still walking. Suddenly a man appears nearby, and moves toward me. He is draped in a large, white towel and wears blue plastic sandals. Perhaps he is coming from the bath. We meet. I ask, "Was that you calling me?"

He stops and turns his head to look at me.

"Yes. It was me calling you. I want you to come here. Say Amen."

"Amen!"

"Say Amen."

"Amen!"

"Say Amen."

"Amen!"

Scene two: Outdoors. It's daytime. The hall opens on to a highland overlooking a green plain dotted with ponds, with a beach to the right where a multitude of fish are magnified in the limpid water. The fish seem so plentiful and so close that I am tempted to reach out and pick one up. I do. It does not struggle in my grasp. The moment I take the fish, my daughter drops from my back like a heavy load and is instantly lost. Till then, I had no idea she was on my back. Her loss is a torment to me. I feel a hand shaking me. I wake and sit up in bed, rubbing my eyes, saying, "*A'uzu billah min al-shaytan al-rajim! Bismillah al-rahman al-rahim!*"

The town lies still beyond my window. The moon seems near. It is brilliant, relief-like, picking out every detail of the rooftops. Every post, every TV aerial, every satellite dish is rinsed in light, enchanted, as if I were still dreaming. A cloud the shape of the head of Nefertiti scurries across the face of the moon and beams with light. I stare mesmerized. The cloud breaks up and reshapes itself into an oil lamp.

"La ilaha illa Allah!" calls the muezzin. *"Allahu akbar!"* The call is taken up by minaret after minaret, magnified in the stillness of the night. I like to think how the call to prayer moves from town to town, from nation to nation, so that *"Allahu akbar!"* moves perpetually over the surface of the earth, just as the last verse of the Qur'an leads to the first, just as the pilgrims in Mecca circumambulate the Ka'aba throughout time.

"Prayer is better than sleep!" cries the muezzin.

"A'uzu billah min al-shaytan al-rajim!" I whisper. I do my ablutions and pray, then enter the room where my husband receives clients. I want to interpret the dream before it fades. I turn on the light and look for one of the big books of dream interpretation until I find it. As I pull it down, three pictures fall to the floor. I stoop down to pick them up and find that two are of Aisha. The Aisha I went to school with. The Aisha on television. My drowsiness flies from my eyes like a startled bird. I sit there on the floor, turning the pictures over in my hands.

On the back is written: Aisha, daughter of Radia. Muhammad, son of Rabha. Sliman, son of Sa'adiya. I also find a slip of paper on which my husband has written the following inscriptions: "Aisha and Muhammad, the lion-hearted. Work to be done that she surrenders herself to him body and soul." Aisha and Slimane, the tottering old man. Work to be done that she will never surrender herself to the lion's heart or to anyone else."

This is what they do then, toying with people's lives. And when God strikes them with drought they pull on their *djellabas* and throng the streets, calling, "O God, provide your servants and your livestock with rain! O God, grant us your mercy and quicken this dead land!" May He provide you with a rain of locusts, you hypocrites! You men who are not men at all!

That evening, I saw them on TV. I saw them, the two of them, Mohammed and Slimane. The first was distributing wheelchairs to handicapped children. The other was inaugurating a new mosque in a neighborhood on the outskirts of town. It was just as I had seen Aisha on that program. The journalist had asked her then whether she had chosen to be single, in order to devote herself to her career.

"It's a big question," she said. "I could write a book on it."

"A book," I said aloud, sitting on the floor, with the pictures in my hands, "the last chapter of which you will never know."

Afterword
by the author

My involvement with writing goes back to when I was in the fourth grade. I was in a private school in Rabat where Arabic and French were the languages of instruction. I loathed reading in French and developed an aversion to using it outside the classroom. This early position against the language of the colonialist proved fortunate, as it kept me from becoming one of the post-colonial Maghrabi writers producing a national literature in a foreign language. My intense aversion toward French may explain why I turned to English as my means of communication with the West.

"But isn't English, too, a colonialist language?" some would ask. Yes, but I have had no confrontation with it. The French put my father in their jails, where he was tortured. French was forced on me and, as Napoleon said, "a language prevails with an army behind it." French threatened to strip me of my native tongue. It was not until 1991 that I became reconciled enough with French to be able to go to France and feel a real desire to speak the language.

I read exclusively in Arabic. I loved my native tongue and was fascinated by its calligraphy. My greatest pleasure as a child was in books. Not surprisingly, I got good marks in composition and dreamed of becoming a journalist or radio announcer, or both.

The first part of the dream came true when I was still an undergraduate. I began publishing articles in Moroccan newspapers and contributing to the Arabic Service of the BBC. Later the dream was fully realized. After university, I began producing a one-hour daily program for the Moroccan National Radio Network. I became a newscaster with Moroccan TV as well. I should have been very happy, but something was missing, and I abandoned my work to take on a new job. At the same time, I started translating Rom Lanau's biography of Mohammed V into Arabic. I well remember the feeling that came over me as I turned the pages of the book. Now at last I felt as if I was putting a finger on what I really wanted. I felt that I was starting to make out the features of a dim dream.

Some time later, I wrote a memoir of the eighteen months I had spent in London in 1968 and 1969 and the result was published in Tunisia. This encouraged me to take a step further and have a go at writing fiction. I began with short stories. Eight were printed in national publications and broadcast by the BBC, and I felt confident enough to begin work on a novel. The year was 1980. I was recently out of work and needed to occupy my time with something. I turned a small room of my house into a study. The project was daunting and at first I felt like someone driving for the first time.

Confronting a blank piece of paper every day was a challenge. I do not remember how much I wrote on the first day but it would be a year of daily struggle before I was finished. Some days I could not go beyond a sentence. Others were spent polishing words and structures.

During that year in my little room I became inhabited by the characters and events of my story, and by its atmosphere and mood. My mind was always at work, searching for the right words. Sometimes they came while I was shopping, or in the car waiting at the traffic lights, or late at night, when I would jump out of bed, go to the desk and write, fearing the words would sneak away before morning.

Perhaps others find the process of writing a novel relaxing, but I did not. It was a difficult task. I dislike superfluous speech by nature, but writing a novel required me to fill stacks of papers as eloquently as I could. In *Year of the Elephant*, I endeavored to drop every word that did not serve some purpose. This explains the book's conciseness and why some Moroccan reviewers have compared it with modern poetry.

Content came easily enough, from the people, places, and events around me. Most of the characters are composites of several real people. Zahra, the protagonist of *Year of the Elephant*, is somewhere between imaginary and real. Women like her existed in the early days of independence, women who fought with their husbands in the resistance movement, only to be later rejected and abandoned for being too traditional, by those same husbands who had joined the new bourgeoisie and now judged their wives unable to keep up. Thus, *Year of the Elephant* reflects an important period in Morocco's political and social history.

Reaction to the book from Moroccan men was hesitant, as if they were not sure what to do with the unfamiliar phenomenon of a woman writer. Some concentrated on the novel's form, and called the style "poetic, easy, pleasant, and attractive, denoting feminine sensitivity and grace, and evidence of a cultured mind, skilled in observation . . . . The text emerges as a fine embroidery of language and emotion."

Those who saw substance beyond form seemed taken by surprise. One asked me, "How is it that you're interested in serious topics?"—apparently convinced that the natural theme for an Arab woman was love. Others were surprised by the verisimilitude of the book. One reader said to me, "I kept telling myself, 'This is true! Why didn't I ever see it before?'" The strangest reaction came from the Middle East where an Egyptian professor said, "She could have been one the best Arab women writers if she were not Moroccan." It seemed that if being a woman was a drawback, being a Moroccan woman was doubly so.

Before long I was asked, "What do Moroccan women think of the book?" In fact, there had been very little commentary from women, save from my circle of relatives who described the book as "beautiful." Women in my culture tend to keep what they think to themselves as a matter of course. As for me, perhaps I had succumbed to the stereotype that women don't speak because they don't think.

Publication of the book in English was undertaken simultaneously by the University of Texas Press and the American University in Cairo Press. It went smoothly and exceeded expectations. *Year of the Elephant* was widely reviewed in the United States and used as a text in American universities and high schools. The most unexpected reaction came from Great Britain, in the form of a poem from professor Sabri Tabrizi from the University of Edinburgh:

You are the voice of many silent voices.
You are the child of your people,
The seeing eyes of the folk.
You set out to tell their stories
And express their heartfelt feelings.

Carry on this track as long as you can.
Remain a child in heart, as far as you can.
We are put on earth to light . . . . And
Shed light on the dark corners of life.

The same year (1989), Elizabeth Fernea from the center for
Middle Eastern Studies at the University of Texas asked me
to write a memoir of my childhood, for an anthology of
childhood narratives from the Middle East. It would never
have occurred to me to write about childhood. Uncovering
one's private life is considered bold and indecent in Arab
society, especially when done by a woman. Nevertheless, I
accepted the offer. Since the memoir was intended for a
foreign audience, I saw it as an opportunity to correct
certain misconceptions about Muslim women. I wanted to
show that as a Muslim woman myself, I was free to take up
a pen and openly express my vision of the reality in my
country. Thus, writing my autobiography became
something of a mission, in fact, a responsibility.

The translation of *Year of the Elephant* was already
clarifying some of the common misconceptions about Islam
and Muslim women, as remarked by Michael Hall from the
University of Melbourne in Australia:

Year of the Elephant stands in sharp contrast to the lurid
images of 'mad ayatollahs' and 'fanatical fundamentalists' all
too common in the Western media and academic discourse

alike . . . . Throughout the text, Abouzeid reinforces an essentially positive image of Islam as a force for social justice and liberation. It is of course unlikely that she set out to challenge negative Western stereotypes about Islam when she wrote *Year of the Elephant*, as the novel was written in Arabic for an Arab-Islamic readership that does not share Western prejudices and misconceptions regarding Islamic religion and culture. Once translated into English, however, the text presents an immediate challenge to Western discourse on Islam, opening the question of the role and value of translation within the field of post-colonial literature.[1]

As one American reader remarked, "I always thought that Morocco was the Morocco of Paul Bowles." Eager to provide a different perspective on my country, I wrote *Return to Childhood* in Arabic and did a literal translation into English. I had been asked to write from fifteen to thirty pages and was afraid I would not even be able to do that. My childhood did not feel like a bubbling source of inspiration. But once I had taken it up, the material began to flow. I was amazed at the details and events that came up from my memory with such clarity and accuracy. This went on for two months, by which time I had filled enough pages to make a book. As I revised the manuscript, I decided the work was valuable and should be published in Arabic too. I contacted an Arab publisher who said, "If only these were the memoirs of Brigitte Bardot!"—confirming my suspicion that I would never have produced them had I had an Arab audience in mind.

I found myself facing a number of problems. Intended for a foreign audience, would not the book's sharp tone and relative openness be judged offensive? I worried about the reaction of my family, in particular, and ended up putting the manuscript in a drawer and forgetting about it for more than two years. When it was published at last in 1993, not only did my family approve, but they were very enthusiastic. The national press and critics as well received it warmly.

Both *Year of the Elephant* and *Return to Childhood* have been subjected to post-colonial or feminist readings. I used to accept the first more readily than the second. 'Women's writing' struck me as a limiting and even derogatory classification. However, as I became better acquainted with the theory of feminist criticism, I discovered, to my surprise, that it seemed entirely applicable to my writing. I realized that if women do belong to a large society where they have the same origin as men, they also "constitute a kind of sub-culture within the framework of that larger society," as Showalter wrote. Women's creative writing would thereby demonstrate a unity of "values, conventions, experiences, and behaviors impinging on each individual."[2]

I discovered that I had been producing women's writing as unconsciously as I had produced a discourse on Islam, not in a quest for any feminist identity or a confrontational crusade to challenge negative stereotypes about Islam, but simply because I had set down my experiences as a Muslim woman.

When writing *The Last Chapter*, again I went through that awe I experienced with *Year of the Elephant*. Talking of something and living it are two different things, like the difference between someone who writes up research and someone who writes fiction. The first has a stack of documents to write from and the second has nothing but a pen and a piece of paper.

Western studies of *Year of the Elephant* emphasized the presence of "the voice of women," "the question of identity," "Islam," "language." Moroccan studies stressed "the non-linearity of time," "legend and politics," "catharsis," "writing specificities."

For me, writing is an ordeal from which I need time to recover; that is probably why I do not write at length. And I am amazed by writers who publish one book after another while having a permanent job, like the Palestinian Ghassan Kanafani and the French Romain Gary, both outstanding writers of the twentieth century. The first was a writer, a politician, and a journalist. The second was a diplomat who published one novel after the other under both his real name and a pseudonym. Both seemed to be in a hurry to say what they had to say before the bell tolled. Both passed away long before their time. Kanafani was assassinated and Gary committed suicide.

When I am writing, I too am afraid that my bell might toll before I get to the end of the book, but I am unable to assume a second job. Moreover, devoting my time to a book ensures that it is completed more quickly. Anyway, I cannot hit two birds with one stone and do not buy that ready-made answer, "I can combine house and office work. It's a matter of organization."

In my society, writing, in spite of its challenges, is seen as unemployment. The truth is that writers are the most content people in these times where notions of materialism and capitalism dominate, because they have chosen a merchandize that has no financial value.

Also, writing in my society is considered tantamount to idleness and an educated woman's idleness is not accepted in Morocco, where people no longer ask a woman whose daughter she is but what she does for a living. This question has been embarrassing to me. If I say, "I'm a full-time writer," people reply, "Yes, but how do you make a living?" "I do freelance work, for foreigners," I tell them, because it is common knowledge that intellectual work in Morocco is not paid for.

Being a woman writing in Morocco is not an overwhelming problem, so long as one can convince the male intellectual institution of the value of one's work. The greatest challenge for me so far has been to be a writer at all.

Leila Abouzeid
at the First Arab Women's Book Fair
Cairo, November 1995

Notes

1. Isobel Armstrong and Helen Carr, *Women: A Cultural Review* (Oxford University Press, 1996), Vol. 6, No 1.

2. Elaine Showalter, *A Literature of Their Own* (Princeton University Press, 1999), p. 11.

Modern Arabic Writing
from The American University in Cairo Press

Ibrahim Abdel Meguid *The Other Place* • *No One Sleeps in Alexandria*

Yahya Taher Abdullah *The Mountain of Green Tea*

Leila Abouzeid *The Last Chapter*

Salwa Bakr *The Wiles of Men*

Mohamed El-Bisatie *Houses Behind the Trees* • *A Last Glass of Tea*

Fathy Ghanem *The Man Who Lost His Shadow*

Mourid Barghouti *I Saw Ramallah*

Tawfiq al-Hakim *The Prison of Life*

Taha Hussein *A Man of Letters* • *The Sufferers* • *The Days*

Sonallah Ibrahim *Cairo: From Edge to Edge*

Yusuf Idris *City of Love and Ashes*

Denys Johnson-Davies *The Naked Sky: Short Stories from the Arab World*

Said al-Kafrawi *The Hill of Gypsies*

Naguib Mahfouz *Adrift on the Nile*

Akhenaten, Dweller in Truth • *Arabian Nights and Days*

Autumn Quail • *The Beggar*

The Beginning and the End • *The Cairo Trilogy:*

Palace Walk • *Palace of Desire* • *Sugar Street*

The Day the Leader Was Killed • *Echoes of an Autobiography*

The Harafish • *The Journey of Ibn Fattouma*

Midaq Alley • *Miramar* • *Respected Sir*

The Search • *The Thief and the Dogs*

The Time and the Place • *Wedding Song*

Ahlam Mosteghanemi *Memory in the Flesh*

Abd al-Hakim Qasim *Rites of Assent*

Lenin El-Ramly *In Plain Arabic*

Rafik Schami *Damascus Nights*

Miral al-Tahawy *The Tent*

Latifa al-Zayyat *The Open Door*